THE LOSTNESS OF ALICE

If I know a song of Africa
does Africa know a song of me?

Karen Blixen
Out of Africa

THE LOSTNESS OF ALICE

John Conyngham

AD. DONKER PUBLISHER JOHANNESBURG

Published by
AD DONKER PUBLISHERS
A DIVISION OF JONATHAN BALL PUBLISHERS (PTY) LTD
P O Box 33977
Jeppestown
2043

ISBN 0 86852 216 3

For Heather, Richard and Sarah

Design by Michael Barnett, Johannesburg
Typesetting and reproduction of text by Book Productions, Pretoria
Cover painting by Heather Gourlay-Conyngham
Cover reproduction by Ince (Pty) Ltd, Johannesburg
Printed and bound by National Book Printers, Drukkery Street,
Goodwood, Western Cape

PART ONE

The Farm

1

She vanished at noon, so they say. One hot midsummer's day, sixteen-year-old Alice Walker left her family's home in suburban Bushmansburg, crossed the lawn to a gate arched with roses and turned into Gatacre Drive, a meandering thoroughfare flanked by large houses in large gardens. Doris Bhengu, the Walker's Zulu maid, was vacuuming in the sitting-room and saw Alice reach the gate. Alice, she said later, was wearing pink shorts and a white T-shirt. Over her shoulders was a yellow towel. A flash of yellow through the hibiscus hedge was the last that Doris saw of Alice.

Shortly before one o'clock, Alice's mother, Margaret, returned from her regular Wednesday-morning game of tennis. Expecting Alice to be home, she called out to her as she entered the house. Dicing carrots in the kitchen, Doris told her mistress that she had seen Alice leave about an hour before with a towel over her shoulders.

'Oh, she's probably gone to swim with Joan,' said Margaret. 'It's lunchtime. She'll be back any minute.' Thinking no more of it, Margaret Walker, feeling sweaty after her game of tennis, had a shower.

At one-thirty Margaret Walker ate a bread roll with cheese and drank a glass of mango juice. At two o'clock, she phoned the Morgans. Joan answered. No, she hadn't seen Alice. She had had a swim and been sunbathing. Try the Jacksons, she suggested. Margaret Walker phoned the Jacksons and their maid answered. No, said the maid, she had not seen Alice. She had been alone in the house all morning.

Uncertain of what to do next, Margaret Walker phoned Duncan, her quantity-surveyor husband, at his office. 'Alice is missing,' she explained, and told him what Doris had said and that she had phoned the Morgans and the Jacksons.

'Don't worry,' said Duncan Walker, 'she'll turn up. I'll see you later.'

Still uneasy, Margaret Walker decided to contact the police if Alice hadn't returned by four o'clock. When the time arrived, she phoned the nearby station and told a young constable about Alice's disappearance. The constable informed her that police policy was to respond only after twenty-four hours had passed since the last sighting of the missing person. Too many reports were false alarms, he said; she's probably with her boyfriend.

'No, she's not,' replied Margaret, knowing that Andrew Thornton had gone home for the Christmas holidays. 'Her boyfriend's at home on his parents' farm near Molteno in the Eastern Cape.'

'But we must still wait,' said the constable. 'If she's not back by the morning, we will get the dog squad.'

When Duncan Walker arrived home at five-fifteen, he was alarmed to find that Alice was still missing. He spoke to Doris who recounted her story, adding something that she had omitted to mention before. Alice, she said, had appeared to be in a hurry. Feeling a sudden burst of panic, Duncan suppressed it and suggested that he and Margaret walk down Gatacre Drive in the direction that Alice had taken. Calling their aged pug, Waldo, the Walkers passed through the arch of roses and set off down the drive behind the hibiscus hedge. 'Waldo,' ordered Margaret, her voice lowered and earnest, 'find Alice!' The pug ignored her injunction and trotted beside his master and mistress.

Some two hundred metres from the Walker home, however, Waldo veered off onto a footpath which weaved through a finger of indigenous bush dividing two suburbs on the hillside above central Bushmansburg.

Margaret remembers telling Duncan: 'If Alice was heading for the Morgans or Jacksons, she may have taken this path.' Edging through the thick undergrowth with its litter of beer cans and plastic packets, Duncan said later that he felt chilled by the possibility that Alice had chosen this tuggled short cut rather than continue up Gatacre Drive to a point higher on the hillside where both suburbs adjoin each other.

Running down the centre of the finger of bush, like the spine down the middle of a leaf, was a stream. Being summer, the stream was flowing strongly and Duncan helped Margaret across, steadying her when she slipped on the smooth wetness of the opposite

8

bank. At this point Waldo became particularly animated and darted into the undergrowth, barking. Apprehensively, Duncan and Margaret followed, slashing a path with their walking sticks. They found Waldo barking at the entrance to a hole dug neatly into the dark earth. Touched by an icy presentiment, said Duncan during his first interview with the press, he prodded the hole with his walking stick and coaxed Waldo towards its entrance. The dog, however, refused and held his ground, barking furiously.

When asked later what they had expected to find, both Duncan and Margaret would not commit themselves. All they knew was that their daughter, Alice, was missing and that their dog, Waldo, was extremely agitated by a freshly-dug hole not far from their home. They found nothing then, however, and assuming it to be an antbear burrow, they returned to the path and continued through the bush to the suburb on the other side. Once there, they called on both the Morgans and Jacksons, all of whom were at home. Both families expressed concern but feigned reassurance and suggested that the Walkers contact the police again before nightfall.

When they arrived home, the Walkers telephoned the local station and were assured by another constable that if Alice hadn't returned by the morning, he would definitely contact the dog squad. 'Those dogs,' he said by way of encouragement, 'will find anything.'

The Walkers spent an anguished evening. Too worried to watch television, they had a light snack, a brandy each, and sat quietly beside the telephone until ten o'clock. Then they drank Horlicks and went to bed, moving the phone to their bedside table. Deeply worried and not wanting to take sleeping tablets, they couldn't sleep. At midnight, Duncan decided to go and look for Alice. He drove around the suburb, not sure what he expected to find, stopping and turning on occasions to throw the beam of the headlights at the screen of foliage through which Alice may have taken her short cut. Finding nothing, he returned home and got back into bed. Margaret was weeping and they lay in each other's arms, neither talking nor sleeping and at a loss as to what to do.

Both remember a storm which broke in the early hours of the morning and drenched the valley. Great rolling roars of thunder and whipping jaggers of lightning filled their bedroom. Still weeping, Margaret crossed to the window in her nightie and watched the sheet of rain in the flashes of lightning. For a while Duncan joined her, awed by the might of the storm and anguished at the thought that his daughter might be out there somewhere in it. While they attempted to comfort each other, both parents failed to realise that the downpour would obliterate any trace of a scent Alice may have left.

The following day dawned grey and low with wreaths of cloud banked up against the slopes of Bushmansnek. While the rain had stopped, the ground was sodden and the undergrowth glistening. At six o'clock Margaret phoned the police and spoke to the same young constable who had promised to alert the dog squad if Alice hadn't reappeared by morning. Had she heard from her daughter? he asked. 'No,' she replied, 'nothing.' 'All right, Madam, we will send a dog,' he said, knowing that the storm would have obliterated the scent, but keeping his promise.

A detective accompanied the dog handler to the Walkers' house. After the Dobermann bitch had sniffed a pair of Alice's denims and been led to the garden gate, it disappeared purposefully down Gatacre Drive with its handler in tow. In the meantime the detective politely grilled the Walkers, jotting in his notebook. On asking who had been the last person to see Alice, and being told that it was Doris, he moved to the kitchen, enquiring and jotting again.

'If she was carrying a towel, could we assume she was going for a swim?' he enquired of Margaret.

'I think so,' she replied, dabbing her eyes. 'Alice's bikini is missing; she was probably wearing it under her clothes.'

'Can you show me the way you think she went?' he then requested, and the Walkers accompanied him down Gatacre Drive on the route that they had taken the previous afternoon.

On reaching the short cut through the finger of bush, the Walkers led the detective into the undergrowth and showed him the hole. Although the downpour had softened the edges of the entrance, the detective seemed impressed.

'Yes,' he said, after squatting briefly and peering into its depths, 'I will get someone to come and dig.'

As they returned up the path from the stream, with cans and packets littering the brush around them, Duncan remembers the detective saying: 'I can see the blacks come and drink here.'

'When they reached Gatacre Drive, they met the dog handler

and his Doberman returning empty-handed from higher up the hill. The detective took the handler aside and spoke to him quietly. Margaret and Duncan remember feeling anxious about their exclusion. The handler then nodded and, calling softly, guided his dog down the footpath from which the Walkers and the detective had just emerged.

Back at the house, the detective again spoke briefly to Doris in the kitchen before thanking Duncan and Margaret. At the front door he reassured the Walkers that he and his men would find Alice.

'Don't worry,' he said. 'Everything will turn out all right.'

Some weeks later he conceded that he had lied. As he left the Walkers that morning he had felt saddened. He knew then, he said, that their investigation would be futile. After decades in the police force he had developed a sensitivity towards each case, an appraisal often at odds with the facts but in which he was usually proved right. Despite his confident facade, as he walked through the arch of roses at the foot of the Walkers' garden that grey morning he was sure Alice Walker would never be seen again.

2

Once the detective had left, Margaret and Duncan moved through to the sitting-room. With nothing to say to each other, they sat in silence. Presently, Doris brought in a tray of tea and biscuits. While Margaret poured the tea, Duncan took a biscuit and began eating it. Margaret remembers being irritated by the sound of his chewing. There was, she said, something too self-indulgent about it. It insulted Alice.

After tea, Duncan said he had to return to the office briefly but would be back for lunch. When she heard the car turn into Gatacre Drive, Margaret phoned the press. If the police couldn't do anything, she decided, then the public should be asked to help. They would understand a mother's predicament.

Sally was at the newsdesk when the telephone rang. She clearly remembers Margaret's words: 'My name is Margaret Walker. My teenage daughter disappeared yesterday. Can you help me?' After letting Margaret tell her story, Sally requested an interview. It would be brief, she promised, but they needed to talk face-to-face and the newspaper required a portrait of Alice. 'Once people see a photograph,' Sally said, 'it will be no time at all before someone recognises her.'

'Come over right now,' said Margaret.

For nearly an hour, the two women sat in the sun-room with its Laura Ashley chair covers and curtains and talked about Alice. Interspersed with sentimental reminiscences and sudden choke-ups of emotion, Margaret related everything she could remember about the last twenty-four hours. Through the window she pointed out the gate arched with roses and the route along Gatacre Drive that she thought Alice had taken. And she pointed across the valley of bush to the suburb where the Morgans and Jacksons lived.

'It should be so simple,' said Margaret. 'Everything happened under our noses.'

'You weren't having any trouble with Alice?' Sally ventured off the record. 'No teenage-parent problems?'

'None at all,' said Margaret. 'The three of us are extremely close.'

'No boyfriend trouble?'

'No-o.' Margaret lengthened the word for emphasis, shaking her head. 'Alice has been going out with a sweet boy called Andrew Thornton. Duncan and I are very fond of him.'

'Where's he now?'

'On holiday in the Eastern Cape. He's a boarder at school here. His family has a sheep farm.'

'Could she have gone to him?' asked Sally.

'I doubt it,' said Margaret, 'although I suppose it's possible. The new term starts next week so she could have waited. And you don't wear a bikini under your shirt and shorts if you're going to travel several hundred miles. A policeman on the phone yesterday asked me if Alice has a boyfriend but we never took it any further because Andrew lives so far away. Perhaps I'd better phone the Thorntons now, in case you don't need to write a story after all.'

Sally sat and waited while Margaret phoned. Andrew's mother answered. From what Margaret said it was soon clear that Alice wasn't with the Thorntons. While recounting the circumstances of Alice's disappearance, Margaret began to weep softly and then hung up. Sally placed a hand on her shoulder and repeated her flimsy assurance that publicity would soon lead to Alice's discovery.

When Margaret had composed herself, Sally left, explaining that she had a deadline to meet but promising to read the story over the phone to Margaret once she had finished it.

When she was sufficiently far down Gatacre Drive to be out of sight of the Walker home, Sally stopped the *Natal Times* car and opened the envelope containing Alice's photograph. Removing the colour portrait, she sat looking at it while the car's engine idled. Although Alice was blonde and blue-eyed and very pretty, there seemed to Sally to be a fragility about her which belied the sensuality of her features. Clearly Alice was no nymphet, but rather a girl on the threshold of womanhood who needed only to wear an Alice band to be a child again. On her return to the newsroom, Sally told Eddie Marx, the news editor, about her interview with Margaret Walker. 'Fuck me,' said Marx, pushing his glasses up the bridge of his nose, 'it doesn't sound good.'

It took Sally an hour to write the story. When she had finished, she read it over the phone to Margaret who was very appreciative and wanted no changes made.

When the night copytaster arrived, Marx told him that a teenage girl had disappeared.

'So what's new?' asked the copytaster.

'She's white,' said Marx.

'Possible front page?' asked the copytaster.

'Yes,' said Marx.

When Margaret saw the story and Alice's photograph on the front page the next morning, her reaction was mixed. While she knew publicity was necessary, she was alarmed by the blunt truth the article represented. Expecting tip-offs about Alice's whereabouts, she stayed at home. The telephone rang incessantly, but not with information. In a display of support, friends and acquaintances phoned to commiserate and Margaret found herself repeating the circumstances of Alice's disappearance many times throughout the morning. By lunchtime, when Duncan returned from the office, she felt numb with anxiety and wanted nothing more than to take a pill and lose herself in sleep.

The police, however, received fewer calls but more information. No-one saw Alice but several people reported sightings of supposedly suspicious people in the vicinity of Gatacre Drive at about noon two days' previously. An elderly widow who lived at the top of the drive saw a black vagrant loitering outside her gate. He was in rags, she said, and looked dangerous. Another resident said he saw an Indian youth on a bicycle. Although two Indian families had recently moved into Gatacre Drive, the cyclist belonged to neither of them. A young boy who was skateboarding in the driveway of his home only fifty metres from the Walker's gate said a deliveryman passed on a motorcycle. No-one, he said, went past on foot. Not even Alice.

'So you see what we are dealing with,' said Detective Sergeant Marais to Sally at the Bushmansberg police headquarters. 'A lot of contradictions.'

3

Several evenings later, Sally was feeling miserable. She was sitting on the verandah eating sweets when I returned to the house from the dairy, my mind filled with thoughts of a dangerously-ill calf. Pulling off my gumboots, I sat down next to her. 'So how're things?' I asked, taking a chocolate from the almost-empty packet in her lap.

'Bad,' she replied.

'Alice Walker?' I asked.

'Yes. The investigation's getting nowhere. The cops are completely in the dark although they're pretending they're onto something.'

'Who, Sergeant Marais?'

She nodded. 'He's all bright and breezy but I'm sure he knows nothing.'

'Unless he's just not saying,' I said.

'But why doesn't he say? We all want to find her. And he needs the press.'

'Maybe the police just lose interest if they can't make progress. They've got too much on their plate these days.'

'I don't know,' she said. 'And I wish I didn't care.' Seeing us, Sally's father, Will, who lived in a cottage at the foot of the lawn, wandered over with a drink in his hand.

'What's wrong, Sal?' he asked with the prescience of a parent. Sally repeated her concern about Alice. 'Remember,' said Will, pointing at his daughter, 'your job is just a job. Leave the world's problems behind at the paper.'

When Sally nodded wearily but said nothing, Will turned to me. 'How's the heifer?' he asked.

'It's dying,' I said and recounted the saga to Sally. I told her how the calf, the offspring of a prize Jersey cow and a straw of the finest imported semen, had developed scours the previous day and how we had treated it with a new drug added to its daily milk ration. After some improvement, the calf's condition had deteriorated; it

15

had become unusually timid, its eyes bewildered and its breathing quick and shallow. But, most alarming of all, it was now wracked by intermittent spasms the frequency of which had increased during the afternoon.

At three o'clock I had phoned the local vet. After being told the symptoms, the drug used and the breed of calf, he had laughed ruefully and diagnosed the cause over the phone. The calf had been poisoned, he said. The drug was to blame. It had been calculated for bulkier Friesland calves; one of its constituents was poisonous above a certain quantity to body weight so although we had followed instructions, we had poisoned our own animal. 'It's finished,' he said, 'but you can wait and see. There's a very slim chance that it'll pull through.' When I protested, he laughed again. 'The pharmaceutical companies won't listen to us,' he said. 'Get Sally to do something in the paper.'

'How horrible,' said Sally. 'I'll definitely do something about it. After we find Alice.'

Will had poured drinks and we sat tippling on the verandah as the sun slipped behind the crags of the Drakensberg. Over in the orchard, the duikers had appeared and were picking their way between the plum and peach trees in search of windfall. In the dam below the terraced rye grass fields, the frogs had begun their evening chorus. Only periodic fits of bleating from the calf pens disturbed the peacefulness.

It was dark when Will returned to his cottage and Sally and I moved indoors for supper. After the television news, when Sally went off to bath, I took a torch and, escorted by Punch and Judy, our two ridge-backs, headed for the dairy. In the vegetable garden, cabbages squatted like damaged chamber pots in the moonlight. Negotiating the steps from the milking parlour, I found the switch and turned on the lights. Rats scuttled away along the rafters. Calves peered over the walls of their pens.

At the end of the row I found the stricken calf on its side on the straw, its eyes wide and tendrils of snot hanging from its nostrils. Only the rhythm of its shallow breathing stopped me from returning immediately to the house for a revolver to end its misery. But, with its delicate beauty attesting to the quality of its genes, I took the craven option and hoped for a miracle. If it hasn't improved by the morning, I told myself, I'll shoot it.

16

Sally was asleep when I got back. After a shower, I made a cup of tea and sat reading the newspaper, appalled and angry at the calf's plight. Shortly before nine the phone rang. I lifted the receiver only to hear the caller replace his. Then I too turned in, slipping into bed beside Sally, enfolding her for warmth.

It was difficult to sleep. With my ears alert for sounds from the calf pens, I dozed fitfully for several hours. Shortly before midnight I was woken by a wild flurry of bleating and the clatter of hooves. The calf, it seemed, was now kicking its metal water bucket. Putting on a dressing-gown, I took the revolver from a drawer in the bed-side table and stumbled to the kitchen door. The dogs were waiting for me, jumping and wagging their tails in the arc of torchlight. Pulling on gumboots, I headed back to the dairy.

Again the calves peered at me over their partitions when I switched on the light. With the revolver cool in the palm of my hand, I moved along the row and found the stricken calf in the last compartment. As before, it was lying on its soiled straw, but now it was dead. With its neck and hind-legs extended, it had clearly died during a seizure. Despite the rigidity of its posture, its immobility suggested peace. Still angry, but also relieved, I retraced my steps to the house. All in all, it had been a bad day. Back in bed beside Sally, I lay wondering about Alice and the calf. Both were gone; at least one was dead. There were parallels, I knew, between the two, but I was too tired to analyse them. Within minutes I was asleep.

4

Five days after Alice's disappearance, the police asked the army for assistance. Doris was sweeping the verandah when several Bedfords ground their way past the Walker home and up to the top of Gatacre Drive. She called Margaret and the two women watched as the lorries disgorged scores of troops who assembled on the verge and were addressed by police and army officers. Their briefing was simple: find the young girl who is lost. In other words, as Alice hadn't been found in the finger of bush where Duncan and Margaret had taken the detective, the net was being thrown wider. This meant that the grassland and pine plantations which covered the slopes immediately above suburban Bushmansburg had to be combed.

'What does she look like?' asked one of the soldiers.

The police and army officers conferred briefly. A police captain dug in his briefcase for the photograph used in the newspaper. Finding nothing, he turned to Sally and several other reporters who were standing nearby and asked if they had a photograph. When they shook their heads, the officer shouted, 'Blonde and pretty, with blue eyes,' at which a murmur rippled through the troops.

As the line of men fanned out along the edge of the plantation, Sally remembers being struck by the vagueness of the briefing. What were the troops expected to find? A torn bikini? A living person or a dead body? A wide-eyed girl, gagged and trussed up on the pine needles or a corpse concealed in a tuggle of brambles? Of course, no-one knew what to expect, but it seemed as if the vagueness of the police was intentional, specifics being too brutal. As most of the troops were married men doing a two-month camp at the nearby Bushmansnek Command, their thoughts must have extended to their own children as they began their advance. Alice, they knew, must be found; not a dead Alice but a make-believe girl who would live happily ever after.

The searchers moved deep into the gloomy colonnade of trunks, followed by Sally and the other reporters. The tread of the troops' boots was muffled by the pine needles and the only sounds were the occasional snapping of twigs and the cries of birds flushed overhead. Presently the troops emerged from the plantation and began to cross a field of chest-high grass. So dense was it underfoot that an order was given for the men to close ranks. At an arm's length from each other, they waded through the matting of stalks. Halfway across the field, the men in the middle of the line broke ranks, shouting that they could smell something rotten. Everyone knew what putrefaction meant, and Sally and the other reporters homed in, fearing the worst.

'What is it?' called men from along the length of the line.

'A porcupine,' shouted the soldier who had first smelt something. Bending forward, he impaled the corpse on a stick and held it above the height of the grass. Everyone around him recoiled from the stench and the sight of maggots seething among the black-and-white banded quills.

Within fifteen minutes the troops had crossed the field of grass and reached another plantation of pines. Finding the going too heavy, Sally and the other reporters had returned to a dirt road immediately above the grassland. Metres before she caught up with the troops who were having a smoke break, Sally noticed a fragment of yellow cloth caught on a thorn in a bramble beside the road. Knowing that Alice's bikini had been yellow, she pointed it out to Sergeant Marais who was standing nearby. He knelt beside the fragment and studied it closely. It had, he noted, been torn from its surrounding material. He noted too that the fabric seemed to be the type used for swimming costumes. Snapping off the bramble stem, he dropped the specimen into a plastic packet as a lepidopterist would, say, a monarch or a swallowtail.

'Thank you,' he said to Sally. 'We must send it to the lab.'

Drawn almost involuntarily, Margaret and Doris walked up Gatacre Drive to a point from where they could watch the soldiers' progress in the distance. They saw the men cross the field. At the consternation over the porcupine – men shouting, gesticulating and converging – Margaret felt a wave of nausea which dissipated into stifled sobs when it became clear that the diversion was nothing.

Once Marais had pocketed the possible clue and those soldiers who had congregated had returned to their ranks, a sergeant shouted orders and the line advanced into the gloom of the next plantation. Together with the other reporters, Sally followed at a short distance, wondering if such resolute combing of the country-side was worth the effort. Alice, she remarked to a reporter from the rival *Daily Herald*, wouldn't be found by anyone who was looking for her. If she was alive she would be sighted by someone who just happened to recognise her from a photograph in a newspaper or on a supermarket notice board. If she was dead, she would be stumbled over unexpectedly; by a wino in a vacant lot, perhaps, or a jogger on a public path, but never by someone looking expressly for her.

Crossing a stream within the plantation, the troops began to climb the adjoining slope. To Sally on the contour road, the sight of a rank of uniformed soldiers advancing through rows of uniform trees suggested mirror symmetry. It was almost, she thought, like looking into a kaleidoscope: trunks and torsos tumbling after each other.

Then, a yell from within the gloom and an agitation of running feet. Once again she and her fellow reporters hurried forward.

'What's happened?' she asked a sergeant.

'A black *outjie*,' he said. 'The men are chasing him.'

It appeared that one of the troops had stepped on a vagrant asleep in a mound of pine needles. Confronted by the multitude of soldiers, the man had grabbed his meagre belongings and darted away among the trunks. A volley of shouts, and all the troops joined the chase, baying in their eagerness.

Minutes later, several men appeared with the vagrant, a dishevelled youth wrapped in rags and with his long hair matted in a grotesque parody of dreadlocks.

'Hey, what are you doing here?' demanded the sergeant in Zulu.

The captive didn't reply. His face was smudged with dirt and his eyes darted from one soldier to another.

'Hey, Bob Marley,' the sergeant tried again, in English, 'did you lose your voice at the disco?' The troops laughed.

'Shall I *donder* him?' a small corporal with a thin blond moustache asked a lieutenant. 'He's not saying anything because he's guilty. I know these *ous*. Where's the white girl, hey, hey?' He prodded the man on the chest with a finger.

'No,' said the lieutenant. 'Take him to the Bedfords. The police can handle him.' Two large soldiers escorted the captive along the contour path towards where the lorries had been parked at the top of Gatacre Drive. As Sally watched them, she felt saddened by the encounter. Why couldn't the troops have treated the man with civility? Was it his proximity to Gatacre Drive? His unkemptness? His blackness?

Sally related the incident that evening. With the milking over, Will had joined us again for drinks on the verandah. The cows were munching hay in the night paddocks between the garden and the dairy. Over in the orchard the duikers were back, picking their way between the fruit trees. An arrowhead of wild duck coursed overhead and hadedahs called from a windbreak beyond the fields of rye grass.

The troops, said Will, were aggressive because they were frightened. The vagrant was a thing of the forest. It reminded him of Kenya: the Mau Mau in the Aberdares and the scattered lights of white farmhouses in the distance. It was just history repeating itself, he added. While the soldiers and their families lay tucked in their suburban beds at night, the dishevelled rastaman loped through the dark trunks, foraging, searching. In the valley below him shone the lights of comfort, the lights of whiteness that had condemned him to the dark.

Although apartheid had been brushed aside and the suburbs were no longer exclusively white, said Will, perceptions hadn't changed. Suburbia was comfort at the rastaman's expense. He was still the beast condemned to the periphery, a man with nothing, and therefore nothing to lose. Unconsciously, the troops realised this. They realised also that with apartheid gone, all of Africa wanted a piece of white surburbia. A piece like Alice, perhaps. With so much to lose, each trooper knew that the rastamen were advancing and many saw themselves as the final line of defence. It was the same situation which had swept through Africa over the last four decades – Algeria, Kenya, the Congo, Mozambique and Angola, Rhodesia, and now the Deep South.

'Let me ask you a question,' said Will, turning to Sally and me. 'Which viewpoint do you think is the more understandable? The troops' or the rastaman's? Not right, just understandable?'

5

As Alice Walker's disappearance developed into a *cause celèbre*, so Sally found herself at the centre of the storm. As the reporter assigned to the story, she was in close contact with both the Walkers and the police and therefore knew as much as anyone of the latest developments. Noting Sally's byline in the paper, many concerned citizens took to phoning her with suggestions. Their interruptions became so frequent that a secretary was used as a filter, only referring Sally to those callers whom she thought had something to offer. Consequently, Sally became a barometer of how the investigations were going. Each evening we discussed developments and I soon found myself thinking about Alice when I was on the farm during the day. I even asked my Zulu labourers what they thought. They didn't have an opinion or they opted not to voice one if they had.

No sooner had Alice's disappearance become public knowledge than a host of theories regarding the case began to emerge. Many whites were convinced that she had been abducted by a black. Conversely, blacks, if they wondered at all, asked themselves why such a fuss was being made about Alice when murders and abductions had long been a feature of black township life. Nothing but the usual police formalities, if anything, resulted from their calls for assistance. Why then should the disappearance of a solitary white girl make front-page news and whip the entire white community into such a state of consternation?

In general, Coloureds were ambivalent but Indians tended to adopt the white perspective. Black men, they felt, coveted white and Indian women so the police should narrow their investigation to black males who had been in the vicinity of Gatacre Drive that Wednesday. An Indian school principal wrote along these lines to the *Natal Times*. Published by the paper, his letter triggered a wide response. Blacks, among them a Catholic clergyman, took exception to the generalisation that black males were abnormally interested in white and Indian women. That premise, the curate felt, was a racist myth. In an ironical letter, a white psychologist at the local university suggested that such a perception on the part of white and Indian males stemmed from a feeling of sexual inadequacy. This bait, flung provocatively at whites and Asians, hooked many readers. A white woman, incensed by the letters of the Indian principal, black priest and white psychologist, wrote a swingeing reply. Indians, she said, were randy because they ate too much curry; good Catholic priests should know nothing about sexuality because they were celibate; white psychologist academics were perverts who sniffed at people's problems at the taxpayers' expense. Her husband, she added in a footnote, was white and sexually very adequate.

Some members of all races were convinced that Alice had absconded with a boyfriend whose identity she had kept secret from her parents. Although Margaret and Duncan Walker refuted such suggestions at least once in the newspaper, those favouring the boyfriend option stuck to it steadfastly. Spirited teenagers, they said, have high libidos and often seek gratification secretly if they think their parents would disapprove. Some of Alice's school friends said she occasionally mentioned a boy other than Andrew Thornton. With Andrew away on holiday, perhaps she was seeing her secret lover. Joan Morgan remembered Alice showing her a photograph of Tom Cruise and mentioning, conspiratorially it seemed on recollection, that he looked like someone she knew. 'I can see her now,' Joan told Sally in a lighter moment off the record, 'lying on a beach in Mauritius with a great-looking guy. The water is bright blue, the sand bright white, and in the palms is a hut where they lie naked together under a mosquito net in the evenings.'

A number of letters, Sally told me, were too offensive to publish, each in its way saying more about its writer than about Alice's disappearance. Some were stridently anti-black while others heaped abuse on the police whom they accused of incompetence. Some even denigrated the state president for a political climate in which whites were no longer safe. The smell of freedom, they said, was too heady for blacks – hence the sharp escalation in violent crime. One unsigned letter said that Alice's voluptuousness was to blame for her abduction. Such girls, said the letter-writer in a juvenile scrawl, were followers of the devil.

Sometimes there were close similarities between letters. On one occasion, Sally received three almost identical letters on consecutive days. Neatly typed on the same typewriter but signed with different names in very similar handwriting, all proved to have non-existent addresses from a particular black area. Their thrust, however, was the same: Alice's disappearance was the beginning of the long-threatened overflow of violence from black townships into traditionally white residential areas. In other words, suburban whites had long had it coming to them and Alice Walker was the first victim. With an eye for falsity honed over the years, the letters editor rejected all three, convinced that they were part of a white rightwing campaign to fan anti-black opinion. However, other apparently genuine anti-white letters were also received. Many of these were published but those considered too offensive were rejected.

One letter, however, was very different from the others. Anonymous and unusually well written, it saw Alice and her disappearance in symbolic terms. Blonde, blue-eyed, fair-skinned Alice, it said, was whiteness personified, a fragile beauty beset by dark forces. From Alice's portrait in the paper, it went on, it was clear that her skin was of that pearly, alabaster caste through which the blue tracery of veins can be seen. Clearly, she was of a breed ill-suited to the harshness of Africa and the rigours of life under a merciless sun, with the air either heavy with damp or dry with a dust that clogs the pores and nurtures blemishes. More beautiful than anything else on the continent, fragile, virginal Alice was a symbol of civilised values of which the only hope of survival, given the odds, was totalitarian white rule. Perceptive enough to see the paradox of such a stance, the writer brushed the awkwardness aside and championed the need for an iron fist to save civilisation. But, the letter continued, now that the state president had capitulated, all the Alices were fair game for the dark forces. South Africa's frontiers were crumbling and whites were beset by famines and plagues and the slow advance of their enemies. If Alice wasn't found, concluded the letter, all was lost.

Although Margaret and Duncan Walker were anxious for any news of their daughter, Sally shielded them from all but the most positive letters. Anything negative or offensive, she considered, would be too hurtful and was passed on to the police on the off-chance that a lead would be found. It occurred to her, said Sally

24

one evening, that if someone had abducted Alice, the culprit may even be reading the letters, excited by the correspondence Alice's disappearance had generated. More sinister still, the abductor, if there was one, may even be one of the correspondents, penning false leads and laughing at the ensuing wild-goose chases.

Either way, such conjecture achieved nothing. Consequently, at dusk each evening, as Sally cooked and I sat in the kitchen talking to her, we arranged to allocate only fifteen minutes to Alice. Thereafter, we discussed other things, chiefly my day on the farm. We spoke about Will's and my activities, the labourers, which cows were on heat or had calved, how the calves were doing and whether we had seen any duikers in the orchard. Sometimes we talked of Will: of what reminiscences had preoccupied him or how breathless he had been on a particular day.

After supper we made a pot of tea and sat reading together in the sitting-room. Then it was time for bed. Sally stayed up late occasionally. I was usually asleep by ten because I had to oversee the milking early in the morning.

6

Quite unexpectedly one morning some months after Alice's disappearance, the editor called Sally into his office and offered her a trip to Kenya. With the repeal of all apartheid legislation, the Kenyan government had opened its doors to South Africans and travel agents were eager to market this new destination. In return for two articles, the *Natal Times* had been offered free trips for a reporter and photographer. Sally, said the editor, was becoming too preoccupied with Alice Walker and should have a break. 'Your farmer friend, Chris,' he added, 'can masquerade as a photographer.'

For the next month before our departure, Sally and I immersed ourselves in Kenya. We grilled expatriates and scoured the local library. Most of the books available were either colonial reminiscences or collections of animal photographs, but we pored over them in the evenings, scribbling notes. An elderly neighbour who had moved south to Natal on Kenya's independence alerted his brother and sister-in-law living near Mombasa and we soon had an invitation to stay with them. With Will looking after the farm, we flew from Johannesburg late one morning, crossing Mozambique but skirting Tanzania where we were still pariahs, and landed in Nairobi towards dusk.

That night in the Norfolk Hotel, our emotions were muddled. Although cosseted by the opulence, we felt strangely lost. Here we were in Africa, we told ourselves, not South Africa, but the real thing. And yet, as in England, we didn't belong. A lifetime of apartheid had cast us adrift.

The following day we saw Nairobi and its environs, then were driven northwards into the highlands. As we weaved from Thika to Karatina to Nyeri so we climbed to a height where even on the equator the nights are cold and the air rings with the clarity of crystal. Sleeping in a former settler mansion, all stone and ivy and tiles, surrounded by acacias and grassland, we sensed all the incongruity of that era with its extremes of privilege and poverty, of tennis parties and Mau Mau blood-letting. At breakfast beside mahogany panelling and a roaring fire, with snowcapped Mount Kenya visible through the trees, it was easy to say: this is not the tropics, this is not Africa. And yet it was and it wasn't. Does a real Africa exist or do we each have our own?

After a night at a game observation post high in the Aberdares, we returned to Nairobi and flew south-westwards across the great trough of the Rift Valley to the Masai Mara. There game abounds and Europeans and Americans enthuse while Africans like ourselves affect a competitive indifference. It was there too, several years earlier, that British tourist, Julie Ward, had been abducted and never seen alive again. Another girl lost. Julie and Alice: both gone, one dead and the other – who knows?

Like timid animals, we grew bolder with familiarity. As we came to realise that our identification as white South Africans no longer implied immediate contempt, many of our doubts were dispelled. At first we were Zimbabweans but later discarded the charade. *Jambo,'* came the ubiquitous greeting, 'are you English?' 'No, South African.' 'Welcome to Kenya. It is good that we are friends now.'

After a week in the interior we flew to the coast. As the plane headed eastwards, with Kilimanjaro across the border to our right, I noted the jottings in my diary – a mixture of colonial relics (Karen Blixen's home; Baden Powell's and Jim Corbett's graves; a deserted coffee planter's house, miraculously intact); and contemporary observations (the majesty of the Masai; the intensity with which the *shambas* are cultivated; and the flowing beauty of the colobus monkeys in the Aberdare treetops).

'I wonder if there's been any news of Alice?' Sally asked as the Indian Ocean appeared and we swung earthwards towards Mombasa airport.

As we reached the door of the plane, so the humidity hit us. The air was still and moist and sheened everything with waxiness. Palms, giant mango trees, casaurinas and bouganvillaeas jostled for space amid the tropical luxuriance. A taxi took us over potholes and decaying buildings to the city on the island. There we toured the old harbour and Fort Jesus, the striking sixteenth-century Portuguese redoubt that dominates the entrance to the port. Mombasa, we thought, is like Durban, only seedier. What Durban will become in a decade or so.

In the afternoon we headed south, crossing to the mainland by ferry and on through the palm plantations and mud villages to the flashy entrances of the tourist hotels. There, among that world-within-a-world where European sunseekers bask in their droves, the driver took a bumpy track between banks of bougainvillaea to a large, double-storeyed house encircled by verandahs. Parking beside a rusting Rover, he demanded payment before wresting our luggage from the boot and leading the way across a bricked court-yard. 'Major Leonard's house,' he announced, knocking on the front door.

It took James and Margery Leonard several minutes to respond. After the prolonged scrabbling of a key in the lock, the door swung open slowly. Sally and I introduced ourselves and we shook hands with the elderly couple. They were confused at first, and seemed only to register who we were when I stated that we were Andrew Leonard's friends from Natal.

'Oh yes,' said the Major, 'you flew in today from Nairobi. We were expecting you. Come in.' As they stumbled ahead of us down a wide passage, an elderly Somali took our luggage from the taxi driver. 'The spare-room, Abdullah,' said Margery Leonard. She pointed down a side passage. 'You two settle in and we'll see you for drinks on the verandah.'

Abdullah ushered us into a large musty bedroom with comfort-able-looking beds, faded curtains and hunting prints hung haphaz-ardly between sash windows. En suite was a cavernous bathroom the white tiles of which had aged to the colour of old teeth. A free-standing cast-iron bath with a dripping tap took centre-stage, while from the ceiling a translucent gecko watched us as we moved between the lavatory and the basin. Presently, we made our way to the verandah where the Leonards were deep in wicker chairs, drinks in hand, while a coil of mosquito-repellent smouldered on a table between them. On seeing us, James Leonard appeared to begin to stand up, but merely leant forward instead.

'Please sit,' said Margery Leonard. 'Throw the cat off the chair. Her mate was put down this morning and she's a bit depressed. Off, Tess,' she shooed, prodding the tabby with a walking stick.

'What would you like to drink, my dear?' James Leonard asked Sally. 'Please don't ask me for anything we haven't got.'

28

With some hesitation, Sally asked for a gin and tonic and I asked for a beer. Seemingly approving of our choice, the Major called Abdullah for a beer from the fridge and slopped gin into three tumblers. As he probed in the ice bucket with a pair of tongs, I noticed how his hand shook and his head bobbed gently. He took a long time with the drinks, and with Sally and Margery Leonard talking beside me, I stared past him at the garden with its rank grass and spindly coconut palms, some of whose trunks had crossed like the necks of courting swans. The sound of the waves drifted up from the darkness at the foot of the lawn and lights from a nearby hotel, smudged by the humidity, winked through a file of casaurinas.

Predictably, the conversation was somewhat strained at first, being no more than the Leonards' queries about our trip and the wellbeing of James's brother in Natal. Several drinks later, however, the decorum began to evaporate. As both James and Margery became more tipsy, so they became more dogmatic, haranguing the Kenyan government for corruption and regretting their decision not to move to South Africa after independence. They had apparently been forced off their coffee farm near Kiambu a decade previously. A cabinet minister, said James, had wanted the place and made it impossible for them to stay on.

'And take here, for example.' James swung an arm expansively at the house and garden. 'We have water cuts every few weeks and the electricity's always going off. They can't run a thing without messing it up. Look at the roads – just bloody potholes.'

'The hotels,' said Margery, 'have their own electricity and water plants, and they tar their own roads, and they still get taxed to high heaven by the government.'

'Africa,' said James with even greater vehemence, 'is a bloody cock-up. But you chaps down there are still all right.'

Abdullah struck the gong in the dining-room. James got shakily to his feet and nearly tripped on a threadbare kelim, grasping Sally's arm for support. More composed, Margery led the way and I heard her talking in what I assumed to be Swahili in the kitchen.

The dining-room was narrow and dark with a long table down its centre. On the walls were tapestries and sombre family portraits in gilt frames. With each of us seated at a different side of the table, we were far apart and each had our own set of silver condiments. There was about the setting a lack of cohesion, as if our separation was so great that we were almost four people eating alone.

As we were about to sit down, James asked me to open the wine. While I wrestled with the corkscrew, he announced, 'It's only Kenyan plonk,' and, extending his tongue slightly over his lower lip, exhaled with a prolonged farting noise. 'It's nothing like your stuff. Andrew once sent us a box of some Cape cabernet sauvignon. Bloody good.' He now inhaled dramatically in a low whistle of approval, before stabbing a ball of butter and smearing it across his melba toast.

As I poured the wine, Abdullah appeared in white from the kitchen with the hors d'oeuvre of curried eggs. 'We've got our fair share of problems down south,' I said. 'There's a lot of uncertainty among the whites, and high expectations among the blacks. We only hope that we can all sort it out.'

'You must keep control,' James said, 'because the rest of Africa is a bloody cock-up.'

Wanting, she told me later, to both get a story and to steer the conversation away from politics, Sally began to ask questions about colonial Kenya. With both the Leonards able to remember Karen Blixen, Denys Finch-Hatton, Josslyn Hay, the Broughtons, and many others, Sally asked for impressions. Without exception, James Leonard dismissed them all as either amoral misfits or sexual deviants, or both. Delves Broughton, he added conspiratorially, a fragment of curried egg at the corner of his mouth, didn't himself murder Josslyn Hay as *White Mischief* had made out, but had hired an assassin to kill him.

At one point during a vehement fit of denigration, James Leonard lurched too far to one side and his chair toppled over. Being busy with my food at that moment, I looked up at the crash and found him gone. Both Margery and Sally sprung to their feet and I ran around the table. Still in his chair, James was lying on the parquet floor with his head and shoulders under the sideboard. When I was unable to lift him alone, Margery called Abdullah and we managed to right the chair with James in it. Throughout all this, he remained silent, and once he was vertical again resumed eating, unaware that blood was trickling from a small wound near his temple. One of the arms of his chair had come partly adrift and was dangling awkwardly like a broken limb.

We continued as if nothing had happened. James was subdued

for several minutes, with Margery watching him concernedly from across the table, but soon the momentum was regained. From time to time he slumped slightly to one side and appeared to seek with his elbow the armrest that was no longer there. At this, Margery would say 'Sit up please, darling,' which he would ignore, firing a question about South Africa at either Sally or myself. Having last visited the country in the sixties, he was way out of touch. Clearly, he was unable to grasp that the country he remembered no longer exists.

It was late when we moved through to the sitting-room for coffee. Abdullah set a tray on a Zanzibari chest and Margery poured while James slumped in a rocker. Beneath another array of family portraits interspersed with watercolours of the Kenyan landscape, Margery, Sally and I nattered until James began to snore softly. Then, as if on cue, we dispersed for bed, leaving him asleep in the dark sitting-room.

Back in our room, Sally and I burst into nervous laughter. What we had imagined would be a decorous evening with two relics of colonial Kenya had been very different. Marooned by their inflexibility, the Leonards were floundering. Only their loathing of modern Kenya sustained them. Living in what seemed to be genteel poverty amidst the clamorous heat and humidity of the tropical coastline, they were rotting with their threadbare carpets, mildewed paintings, foxed books and antique furniture swollen with damp. It was a case of adapt or die, and they were dying.

Hot and sweaty, we filled the large cast-iron bath and submerged ourselves in the cool water. After discussing the Leonards' predicament, we washed each other, lingering at our points of arousal until our rising passion propelled us to a wet coupling, watched only by the gecko. Then it was bed. As we lay on the sheets in the darkness, just conscious of the delicate spiciness of the mosquito repellent and the soft rushing of the waves, so we drifted into sleep.

Early next morning, Abdullah woke us with tea. No sooner was the sun above the horizon than the heat was drumming on the roof and slicing through the curtains. While Sally worked on her diary, I had a cold bath and shaved. Then she too bathed and we went out to the verandah where we found Margery, looking sprightly in a pastel frock, doing a jigsaw.

'Sleep well?' she asked cheerily, and rang a bell under a carpet with her foot. 'Start with your mango and Abdullah will cook your bacon and eggs.' Sitting at a table covered with a crisp white cloth spotted with darns, we scooped curls of stringless mango with silver spoons engraved with a heraldic crest. A grass blind blocked the glare, and a fan hummed, turning from side to side.

While we ate, we talked to Margery who craned over her jigsaw with her glasses low on the bridge of her nose. 'You should spend the morning swimming,' she said. 'It's hot and there's no wind. Take Lilos and paddle out to the reef.'

Half an hour later, we carried Lilos through the palms to the belt of white sand which appeared around a headland from the north and then wandered southwards into the haze. Fronting the hotels some distance away were gatherings of pink tourists sunbathing and swimming while black youths wandered among them, touting curios.

Wading through the shallows, we swam out with the Lilos and then lay on them, our closed eyes dancing with sunny patterns. With the water lapping against the inflated canvas, it was very peaceful and I stretched out and drew Sally's Lilo alongside mine, resting my face against her neck and feeling and smelling her cool flesh warming in the sun. From time to time we slipped into the water, either swimming some distance across the mottled blues towards the white line of the reef, or returning soon to the Lilos where we resumed our sunbathing. As we lay and baked I kept one eye on our bundle of possessions on the beach and the other on Sally beside me, tall and snug in the cusps and puckers of her tanga. Only at noon, with the heat exploding above the water, did we paddle ashore and weave up between the palms to lunch.

Reaching the house, we found Margery still at her jigsaw, poised like an egret above the patchy mosaic. Beside her in a wicker chair was James, a plaster on his temple, listening to Chopin on the BBC World Service and reading a back issue of the *Spectator*. Greeting us enthusiastically, he crossed to the drinks table and without asking poured four generous gins, topping them with tonic and clusters of ice.

'I've just heard on the radio,' he said, 'that there's been a bit of trouble down your way. The Zulus are clobbering the Xhosas on the mines. Your police should just cordon off the area and let them get on with it. You two want to have a shower? There's one down the passage. Finish your drinks and I'll fill you up before you get back.'

We showered, soaping off the salt residue and washing our hair. Naked afterwards in the bedroom, our heads brushed lightly by the gin, we felt blissfully cool, our breathing slow and rhythmical and our shoulders smarting slightly from sunburn. Then, both of us dressed in white short-sleeved shirts, baggy shorts and sandals, we returned to the verandah.

'We've got a proposition,' said James, putting down his magazine. 'Margery and I have a house on Lamu, the island off the north coast near Somalia. We haven't been there for years but our daughter, Jenny, and her family use it for a month each year and we hire it out occasionally. If you two get yourselves up there, we'd love you to use it and report back on how things are. We've got an old Swahili fellow keeping an eye on it. He's never let us down, but you never know. And you should find it an interesting place.'

As we had several days to spare, we didn't take much persuading. Throughout a succession of gins and a searing curry we discussed the island, James and Margery doggedly trying to sell us what we had already bought. After lunch Margery assumed responsibility for the travel arrangements and wrestled tipsily with the telephone as James sank slowly into a stupor. Abdullah brought tea and on Margery's instructions Sally stirred and poured.

'They call Lamu the Katmandu of Africa,' said Margery, dropping the receiver to her side momentarily before resuming her conversation. James began to snore and Sally and I sat listening to his snorts and whistles.

'It's all arranged,' said Margery at last, clattering the receiver back onto the phone. 'You fly from Mombasa tomorrow morning. You can pay for your tickets at the airport.'

'Thank you very much,' Sally and I said simultaneously.

'Darling, I wish you'd sit up straight,' Margery exclaimed, looking pointedly at James who had subsided deeper into his chair and was snoring loudly.

The three of us drank our tea before retiring for a siesta. As Sally and I headed down the passage, Margery shouted after us, her voice elastic with drink: 'Sleep tight. See you at tea-time.'

In the bedroom we drew the curtains and collapsed on our beds. Through a tear in one of the curtains I could see the palms and, beyond them, the sea, all ablaze with heat and light. Sally was soon asleep. For a time I lay and watched her. Then I closed my eyes. 'Why Katmandu?' I remember thinking before I too slipped away.

We emerged heavy-headed several hours later and found Margery still hard at work at her jigsaw. Again her foot tapped the bell-button beneath the carpet and again Abdullah appeared with tea.

Shortly before dusk we went for another swim. Forsaking the Lilos, we waded through the shallows and swam out to a small raft to which a number of dinghies had been moored. We climbed aboard and with the gentle swell sucking beneath us watched the garish hotel lights become brighter as the darkness deepened. Music burst from the buildings and a breeze wobbled the silhouettes of palms against the stark white facades. Beside all the towering brightness, the Leonards' property was dark and wooded, with several lights flickering through a screen of foliage. New Kenya and Old Kenya, we thought, juxtaposed

As we swam back towards the beach, an hotel band struck up a particularly throbbing number and the sound only diminished once we had passed the file of casuarinas and weaved up through the palms to the Leonards' house. Unsurprisingly, Margery was still at her jigsaw. Sally noticed that she had changed her dress and her hair was brushed. James had reappeared and was reading a Western. Glasses of gin squatted beside them and the pungency of the mosquito repellent was almost tangible in the humid heat. Again they greeted us cheerily and James offered drinks. We declined temporarily and slipped indoors for a shower.

'We must have a good chat tonight,' James said before we headed down the passage to the guest room.

Compared with the previous evening, our last supper was a relatively sedate affair. Although the Leonards were ticking even before we moved through to the dining-room, there was none of the previous evening's acrobatics. James was unusually outgoing before the telltale signs began to emerge: his nodding became more frequent and he slumped back in his damaged chair and began snoring softly. Not bothering even to mention her husband's withdrawal, Margery spoke at length about Lamu and how much they had enjoyed their holidays there in the old days. At the height of the Mau Mau, she and the children had been moved to the relative safety of the island, leaving James up-country on the farm, toting his rifle on his rounds between the coffee bushes.

'Those were difficult times,' said Margery with a wry smile, 'but we survived. It'll take more than the Mau Mau to get us.'

We packed before bed and Sally worked on her diary while I fiddled with my borrowed camera and checked the rolls of film which I had taken since our arrival at the coast. Then we slept, our suitcases and hand luggage stacked expectantly at the foot of our beds.

Abdullah woke us shortly after dawn. We hurried our ablutions and then drank our tea in front of the open windows, watching the morning's blaze intensify and the tentacles of heat breach the barrier of foliage and encircle the house. Margery was on the verandah when we appeared, chivvying Abdullah and working at her interminable jigsaw. Joining us for breakfast, she repeated her Lamu instructions and thrust into my hand an elementary map of the island.

'That's our house,' she said, pointing at a red cross amidst the labyrinth of alleys in Lamu town. 'You can't miss it. Walk up from the quay towards the fort and look on your right for the most beautifully ornate door imaginable.'

Just then, Abdullah appeared with a telegram. 'It's for you two,' said Margery, giving it to Sally. Chilled, Sally opened it and read slowly: 'Alice's bikini bottom found in bush by Walker's dog. Investigation revived. Marais says hello. Have fun. All well at home. See you at airport. Will.'

'Not bad news, I hope,' said Margery. As Sally hurriedly explained the Alice Walker saga, I cursed Will for intruding. We had contrived to leave Alice far behind, but here she was again. While Sally seemed delighted by the breakthrough, if it was one, Waldo's discovery filled me with foreboding. If Alice had been wearing her bikini under her shorts and shirt when she left home that morning, then how had she become separated from such an intimate article of clothing? On our return, when I chided Will for sending the telegram, he pleaded innocence: Sergeant Marais had insisted that Sally should know. And knowing that Sally was a major player in the investigation, he, Will, had felt compelled to pass on the news.

As Sally was completing her explanation, Abdullah appeared again to report that the taxi had arrived. 'You get yourselves ready,' said Margery, 'and I'll get James.'

We were assembled near the taxi when James surfaced. At the sight of the elderly man in his paisley dressing gown and slippers the taxi driver's irritability dissolved into obsequiousness as he bowed and scraped in a succession of *salaams*. Wanting to get a photograph of the Leonards before we left, I positioned them with Abdullah beside the front door including, at the last minute, the taxi driver who, mortified at his exclusion, was suddenly all grins, as the subsequent photograph showed. It was a quaint tableau: the sleepy Colonel Blimp and his feisty little wife, the kindly fezzed factotum and the Cheshire-cat driver. Like the cast of some amateur farce, they seemed to be hamming it up for the photographer.

After hurried goodbyes, and thank yous, and promises of letters, we left the Leonards and Abdullah and bumped between the bougainvillaeas to the main road, then swung right towards Mombasa.

7

You can't imagine how difficult it is piecing together these fragments from a lost world. Like porcupine quills sunk in flesh, each has to be painstakingly extracted to limit the pain. There is about the task the intricacy of surgery: incisions, tucks, pleats and then the delicate suturing, end to end, of one sentence to another. Or that is the intention. Sometimes the mechanics go badly wrong and moods gush through the lines, requiring emergency stanching. And, behind it all, is the pulse of the narrative, that steady rhythm which must be kept alive to prevent the flesh from rotting.

Far below I can see warships riding the swell in the harbour – great grey brutes straining at their leashes. Seagulls skein down from the rocky heights, their wings riding the currents and their eyes as sharp as diamonds. Whenever I throw a crust onto the verandah, it is snapped up in seconds. But the set piece outside is an elemental collage of land, sea and sky. I study it through the window while the fire rages within me.

Alice. Like a pall, she's here now as she was on Sally's and my first excursion into that other Africa. An omnipresent non-presence. It's not only the Walkers who suffer so intensely. Sally suffers too and, through her, me. Before long, you will know the answer, for what it's worth, but for now your job is the slow accumulation of details, like the accretion of silt on the bottom of the stillest pond, and my task is to lead you on.

Back to Kenya, that is.

Our flight from the airport to Lamu's neighbouring Manda island was scheduled to take an hour. Rising above Mombasa's rusting roofs and towering mango trees, our small plane arced northwards and followed the coastline. With the lowlands on our left and the Indian Ocean to our right, we whined high above the beach, passing Kilifi and Malindi, and landed on Manda's earthern airstrip midway through the morning.

Catching a motorised dhow across a choppy sound, we peered

through bursts of spray as Lamu town advanced from a strip of castellated and verandahed buildings serrated with palms to a promenade bustling with robed figures and burdened donkeys. At a quay, we clambered ashore, immediately enchanted by the island's Arabian and African mix. This was Africa as we had never seen it before. Black-robed Swahili women, their faces half-concealed, melted into the shadows of the narrow alleys while groups of men wearing white robes and fezzes talked and laughed in the blast of sunlight. Unknown to us only two days previously, here was Africa's Greek island of sorts, a speck of exotica moored to Kenya's coast. With no motorised vehicles, Lamu had resisted much of modernity and baked quietly in the heat, stitched to its palms and minarets by the cries of its muezzins.

Following Margery's directions, we headed away from the quay, transfixed by the muddle of beauty and squalor: quaint coral-walled alleys aslink with diseased cats and exquisitely carved doors inches from open sewers. In an alley near the town square with its Beau Geste fort and giant almond tree, its stoic donkeys and bustling stalls, we found the Leonards' house, knocked on its door and waited until the elderly caretaker appeared. I passed him Margery's note and he read it intently.

'We have come from Major and Mrs Leonard,' I ventured.

'I know,' said the old man. '*Bibi* phoned this morning. Come inside.'

Leaving the vibrancy and heat behind we passed through a dark room into a cool Italianate courtyard encircled on several storeys by verandahs and centred by a palm which rose from among patterned tiles to way above the rooftop.

'*Bwana* Leonard is well?' asked the caretaker.

'Yes, very well,' I lied.

'That is good.' After a pause, he continued: 'Let me show you the house. It is very old. Nearly two hundred years.'

Leading us from storey to storey, the old man revealed the house's intimacies: its rooms opening onto the courtyard; its floors cambered to disperse monsoon rainwater; its secluded *zenana*, through the latticework of which the women once peered; its ornate four-poster beds clasped snugly by alcoves; its niches in the high walls, each filled with a delicately patterned porcelain plate or bowl; and its flat roof, partially canopied with palm thatch, from which much of the island could be seen.

Here, I thought, is an enduring African artistic heritage. Like Egypt's pyramids, the Bushman paintings in the Drakensberg and Great Zimbabwe's ruins, some Swahili artefacts had durability. While there were shacks on the periphery of Lamu town, those urban villas were no transient mud huts, but lasting examples of functional beauty. For someone haunted by impermanence, such a realisation was hugely reassuring.

Once he had showed us around, the caretaker asked if we wanted him to make us supper that evening. When we declined, he gave us a key to the front door, then disappeared. Early in the afternoon we went out, eating at a quay-side taverna and then taking a motorised dhow several miles along the island to Shela, a picturesque hamlet of white-washed houses and palms. There we swam at an extensive stretch of beach backed by dunes reputedly containing the bones of neighbouring islanders killed in a battle with the Lamuans early last century.

Towards the end of the afternoon, we headed back to a jetty on a headland where the dhow called hourly. On cresting a dune, we surprised a couple copulating. Both were young, she a European and he a Swahili youth. As we skirted them, decorously averting our gaze, the tempo of their motions increased suddenly until she cried out ecstatically in German and he reciprocated with repeated barking grunts.

'I hope they've got a condom,' said Sally when were sufficiently far away, and we laughed.

Apart from the helmsman, there was no-one else on the return journey to Lamu town. As he stood in the stern, dextrously steering his dhow with a foot on the tiller, the implications of that coupling behind the dune occurred to us. With East Africa's population supposedly riddled with the Aids virus, tour operators warn all tourists of the danger of intimacy with the locals. Conceding that the 'bonkers', as we called them, could have been a monogamous couple of long standing, it was more likely that the girl was a tourist and the youth a Lamuan whom she had met during her stay. If that was the case, wasn't the girl being a bit reckless? Yes, we agreed, but Sally had a novel explanation.

'That girl,' she said, 'is the new imperialist. No longer is it European men with pith helmets subjugating African men and having their women. Now, in the age of first-world gender equality, European women travel to untamed Africa and have it off with well-endowed black men. For the more adventurous, Aids is no deterrent. Like their male forebears, some will die from the rigours of foreign service, but the rewards to be had make it well worth the risk. Modern Europe is too tame. Some people need to take chances. That girl coming behind the dune was living out her fantasies. For a sum, or more likely nothing, she could make that youth do whatever she liked, and then discard him and go home. Compared with the thrill of that, Aids is nothing.'

'So,' Sally continued, 'the quest for Prester John becomes the quest for Mister Dong.' And we laughed again.

Although we didn't admit it during the journey back to Lamu town, our sighting behind the dune had aroused us both. As repressed South Africans, such a joyful example of miscegenation had fired our imaginations, making us promise each other that something special would happen on our four-poster bed later that evening. When we reached the house, the caretaker was there, talking to a friend in the scullery. We bathed and relaxed in a variation of Morris chairs with leg-rests that swung out from under the arms. The caretaker bought us beers and we lay back in great comfort with our legs raised like lazy gynaecological patients, Sally updating her diary and me reading about the island in a guidebook. As the rays from the setting sun created oblique shadows in the courtyard, I attempted unsuccessfully to take several interesting photographs. I realised then that with my ineptness as a photographer, I would have to justify my trip merely with snapshots of the sights. Artistic photographs were beyond me.

Soon after dark, we went out to the taverna beside the quay. Nothing more than a row of tables and chairs under a palm thatch roof, it resounded with soul and Motown and attracted a largely foreign clientele. As we drank our beers and ate a tangy vegetable curry, we watched the backpackers, guessing their nationalities and backgrounds. Young and attractive, most of them seemed European or American, successors to the flower-children who had flocked to Lamu in the sixties. Hence, we supposed, Margery's Katmandu reference. Being in our early thirties, Sally and I seemed old beside them.

We looked in vain for the 'bonkers'. 'They're probably at it in some shuttered room,' said Sally, reminding us of our own intention. We paid and walked circuitously through the dark alleys, itching with expectation.

Back at the house, the caretaker was nowhere to be seen. Following a trail of muted lamps, we found our large four-poster veiled in a mosquito net, its sheets turned down and an insect repellent smouldering beside it. We began to undress, tossing our clothes onto an ornate kist. Near the mosquito coil I noticed a *coco de mer*, that large coconut seed-pod which so closely resembles a vulva, complete with its intricate pattern of pubic hairs. The sight of it heightened my ardour and I hurried Sally beneath the veil and onto the bed. Snapping off the lamps, we began to kiss in the moonlight and smooth our hands along the contours of each others' bodies. As our momentum increased, so each sought the other's intimacies in a mutual caress, my head buried in the scent of her thighs while her pursed lips went about their business. Soon came the mad need for fusion and a hurried positioning before the urgent rhythm began. Near the height of our passion, as if possessed, we uncoupled briefly and feverishly tore a hole in the mosquito net before resuming our lovemaking through it like a wanton Pyramus and Thisbe in *A Midsummer Night's Dream*. Then came the acceleration to deep, shuddering cries; then subsidence.

With the madness dispelled, we fell asleep in a moist embrace. Not long after midnight I was awoken by the cries of a muezzin. Lying in the darkness, rocked by Sally's gentle breathing, I began thinking of the farm: of Will and the labourers; of how many cows had calved in our absence; of the duikers in the orchard. As I dozed off, Sally suddenly began to whimper and then thresh about. Feeling her nails snatch at my shoulder, I clasped her to calmness and demanded to know what was the matter.

'It's Alice,' she sobbed. 'She was in a harem. Three men were abusing her. She was screaming as they tossed her about like a doll.'

'Don't worry, Sal,' I said, holding her tightly. 'You've been dreaming. It's probably just the sound of the muezzin who's been calling.'

But Sally was inconsolable; for nearly an hour she shivered in my embrace until we drifted off to sleep again.

We spent four days on the island. It was idyllic but overshadowed by Alice. In a way, she was the trip. Had she not disappeared and

Sally not been ordered to hound her searchers, and become over-wrought in the process, a more senior journalist would have been given the Kenyan assignment. But there we were on Lamu, swimming and sleeping and loving like a couple in another age, enveloped by the timelessness of the beaches, coral walls, palms, dhows and the devotions of Islam.

Hiring a dhow to visit ruins on neighbouring Pate and Manda islands, we felt ourselves so adrift from everything that the sight on the horizon of an Arab slaver low with plunder, or a Portuguese caravel riding the monsoon from Goa to Mombasa, or a brisk British gunboat on patrol, would have seemed unremarkable. In the heat of the sun, the endless vista of blue water fringed by a green-and-ochre coastline and the Swahili banter of the crew, there was something elementally reassuring. Here was a landscape forged over aeons, and a hybrid people who belonged in it.

On the day we left it was raining. We crossed the sound huddled under a tarpaulin and took off among the dunes with the aeroplane's windshield wipers flicking aside the drizzle. Crossing the hinterland en route to Nairobi, we exchanged the sea for semi-desert and then the towering escarpment. Killing time at Kenyatta airport, we scribbled and read until the South African Airways airbus taxied into sight through the glass.

As we filed into the aircraft cabin, we entered another world. While the piped music was blandly international, the pretty, over-made-up hostesses were unmistakably South African. And with the subliminal confusion of kinship, both Sally and I warmed to them immediately. For all greater Africa's wonders, it was clear that we were glad to be returning to that fractious limbo which we called home. Only hours separated us from Will and the cattle and the place where three months previously a girl had gone for a walk and vanished into thin air.

8

It was good to be back on the farm. Seven cows had calved during our absence and the duikers were still foraging daintily in the orchard. Will was breathlessly eager to know everything about Kenya. Were Nairobi's jacarandas still standing? Were there still aviaries in the Norfolk's inner courtyard? Had the country been destroyed? Yes, yes and no, we replied. As we sat on the verandah on our first evening back, with the sun dropping behind the distant peaks of the Drakensberg, both Sally and I felt an upsurge of well-being. It is good, we thought, to be back in our Africa. Like the former settler mansion in the Aberdares and the Leonard's home south of Mombasa, it wasn't what outsiders would call the real Africa, but it was real enough to us.

Alice, however, remained as elusive as ever. Despite the discovery of part of her bikini, the investigation was still floundering. With forensic tests providing no new information, all that could be construed from the find was one of three things: that she did take the short cut through the finger of indigenous bush; or she was taken into the bush after her abduction, if indeed she had been abducted; or her bikini bottom had been deposited there after it had been removed by herself or a person or persons unknown.

There was also, of course, a more sinister aspect. As Marais remarked to Sally once they had resumed their morning meetings at the Bushmansberg police headquarters, the case for foul play had been strengthened. It seemed highly unlikely under the circumstances, he said, that Alice would have abandoned such a garment willingly. For this reason, the police had played down the discovery. To retain the public's help, Alice had to remain a beautiful teenager whose reunion with her parents everyone could look forward to enjoying. Any suggestion that she was no longer alive had for now to be suppressed. The Walkers were to be told no more than was reported in the press: that is, that such a discovery of clothing augured well for the investigation; in short, that headway was being made at last. To tell them the truth at this stage, said Marais, was counterproductive.

'But what if she had met a lover?' asked Sally. 'Couldn't that account for the removal of her bikini?'

'It could,' said Marais, 'but I don't think that this is a case of joyous lovemaking under the trees.'

Ever since Sally's first article about Alice's disappearance, she had been inundated with letters. And although it was now four months later, the supply was as strong as ever. While most letters merely contained suggestions or support, some were from psychics with offers of assistance or specific instructions.

The opinion of more than eighty per cent of the letter writers was that Alice had been abducted rather than absconded. Almost all were convinced that the culprit was a male and most white correspondents thought it was a black male, although Indians and Coloureds were also accused. Very few whites conceded that someone of their own racial group might be guilty. Most Indian and Coloured correspondents were divided on the abductor's race. Blacks, however, were sure it was a white.

A group of liberal whites suggested that while a white male was probably to blame, he had chosen the time and place carefully in an attempt to suggest that blacks had been involved. Since the abolition of influx control and the Group Areas Act, Gatacre Drive had become a thoroughfare for blacks wishing to cross to the neighbouring suburb via the finger of indigenous bush. The disappearance of a teenage white girl at such a time and place was most likely to incriminate a black male trespasser. This, said the liberals, was what the white criminal wanted everyone to think.

In short, in all but a handful of letters, the writers did little more than betray their own prejudices. As products of a long-segregated society, no-one seemed able to rise above race and scrutinise the case objectively. Does pure objectivity exist, asked Sally, or are the findings of investigations always just the sum of the prejudices of their participants?

The publication of Alice's photograph generated a different, if equally wide, response. Now it was a case of heads and tails, of matching a portrait with its subject. Many readers reported sightings. Someone had seen Alice hitchhiking near Kimberley, hundreds of kilometres away from Bushmansburg; another had seen her among the slot machines at the Wild Coast casino; a third, a Cypriot sailor whose ship was undergoing repairs in a Durban dry dock, claimed that Alice was one of a squad of prostitutes who had come aboard one night to service the crew. With nothing substantial to go on, the police followed every lead. So far, none had come to anything.

Nor had the psychics succeeded in making headway. Three said Alice was dead and suggested where her corpse could be found. Two were convinced that she was still alive, one believing that she had run away with an older lover. The other felt that she had been abducted by a white slave ring, based in the East but co-ordinated from Mombasa, which had begun recruiting in South Africa since President de Klerk's reforms had encouraged intercourse with the rest of the continent.

One even claimed that Alice was trussed up in a suburban house and named the street; another that she was dead and had been incinerated in the city crematorium through the complicity of an undertaker; yet another was convinced she had been strangled and her corpse submerged in a fish pond in a garden not far north of the city centre.

Doggedly, the police followed up each lead, Marais handling all those in Natal and delegating this task to detectives in the other provinces.

Everyone drew a blank. Although Marais wouldn't agree, this was not surprising. High expectations, poverty, vengeance and the perception that a reformist government had lost the will to repress, created a heady brew for the discontented. Illegal firearms abounded and crime was rampant. With their resources overextended, the police had new priorities. State survival was paramount. Common crime had been demoted. Who really cares, you could hear them saying, about a teenage girl who has gone missing? Granted, she was white, but there are lots of other girls like Alice.

9

One of my greatest pleasures was ploughing. With the stutter of the tractor gunned to a rhythmic throb, I could sit for hours in the diesel fumes as the shears sliced and tumbled the dark soil. Locked into parallel contours, with one hand compliant on the steering wheel, riding its tugs and jerks, I leaned an elbow on the mudguard and in a slow reverie scanned the surrounding hills. Only cattle egrets, wheeling above my wake like sheets of white paper caught in a thermal, seemed to demand attention. Otherwise, it was just the sound and smell of the tractor and the surge of horsepower in harness.

My thoughts, of course, were filled with Sally. But so deep had Sally immersed herself in the mystery of Alice that the two had become one. Neither Will nor I remained her emotional ballast. Withdrawing from us, she was tethered to the lostness of Alice and went where the case summoned her. When the investigation seemed to be progressing, she was in high spirits. Conversely, when each cul-de-sac was reached, she either collapsed into bed immediately after supper or tippled late into the night on a chilling low.

Every day had its Alice pattern, starting at breakfast. Having returned from the milking, I was usually at the table reading the newspaper when Sally appeared. As she hurried through her muesli and toast, I read aloud her Alice story, bouncing it off her on the rebound and priming her for the sleuthing ahead. Invariably, there was progress of sorts. Even if the trail had run cold, she had the morning meeting with Sergeant Marais to look forward to. Marais, it seemed, brimmed with initiative and his vigour was understandable. What better way for a young and ambitious detective to make a name for himself than to solve a case that had caught the public's imagination? The white public's, that is.

While I went about my farming chores, often with Will beside me in the bakkie or workshop, the Alice momentum began to increase. After heading first to the paper's offices, Sally moved on to the Bushmansburg police headquarters for meetings with the police liaision officer and Marais.

At the daily so-called crime conference, Sally said, the liaision officer began by listing all the violent incidents which had occurred in the Bushmansburg area over the previous twenty-four hours. For example:

06h21: Body of black male, approximately 25 years, found dead beside bicycle at Naylor's Halt. Bullet wound in the head. AK47 cartridges found at scene.
09h46: Asian male, approximately 50 years, killed in hit-and-run accident at corner of Gandhi and Shepstone Streets.
11h32: Black female, approximately 20 years, raped and burnt at Dedela, upper Edenvale.
13h13: White male, approximately 65 years, fell to his death from fifth floor of Springbok Flats, Riverside. No foul play suspected.

And so on. Once this litany of violence was completed and Sally had it recorded in her notebook, she moved down the corridor to Marais' office where the two sleuths put mundanities aside and concentrated on Alice. Marais led, charting the route ahead, while Sally helped with the polishing, suggesting an alteration here, a diversion there. With the next step planned, Sally either returned to the office or accompanied Marais if his movements were considered sufficiently newsworthy. As this co-operation between policeman and journalist was frowned upon by the other detectives, most of whom regarded the liberal press with distrust, discretion had become the watchword. When Marais was working with his associates, Sally kept her distance, but when they were were alone, she said, they worked as one.

'Does Marais now tell you everything?' I asked Sally some way into the investigation.

'Yes,' she replied. 'He is told to keep quiet about some things but he tells me anyway. His superiors don't know how much I know. But he knows that he needs me.'

Sometimes Sally phoned breathlessly from the police station. Agnes, our Zulu maid, called me from the workshop or nearby fields and with Punch and Judy bounding beside me, I ran up through the mire of the cattle pens and past the hedges beside the vegetable garden to the house.

'I'm going flying with Marais,' she said on one occasion, 'so I may be late. A clairvoyant says Alice's body is in a garden pond somewhere due north of Bushmansburg. We're taking a police helicopter to have a look. See you later.'

I was ploughing when they flew over. Despite the roar of the tractor, I could hear the chatter of the rotors before the blue-and-yellow police helicopter appeared over a nearby copse of blackwoods and executed a low arc above me. I waved and could see Sally's arms flailing within the perspex bubble of the cockpit. Then the pilot righted the machine and it receded into the distance towards the Karkloof Hills.

Although they found nothing, Sally was on a high that evening. Drinking glass after glass of riesling, she rattled on about taking off with Marais and a pilot from a pad behind the police barracks and climbing high above the city until even the high-rises resembled building blocks on a nursery carpet. Once airborne, they swung northwards and scoured the four gullies that radiated into the surrounding hills north of the city centre. Beyond the spread of suburbia, a ring of smallholdings appeared before the divisions dissolved into the openness of farmland.

Something in the clairvoyant's instructions had intimated a location neither urban nor rural and it was therefore in the peripheral smallholdings belt that the pilot was instructed to search. As he manoeuvred the helicopter up the gullies and over the encircling ridge of hills, at times barely above towering pines and gums, Sally and Marais peered through the perspex for any sign of a garden pond. While swimming pools and small dams were common, only two ponds were located, both dappled with water lilies at the foot of large, old gardens. These Sally marked on a topographical map of the area, noting the exact position and the meanderings of the access roads.

Once the wooded slopes of the Bushmansberg had been scoured, Marais instructed the pilot to search the farmland further north of the city. Clairvoyance, he must have thought, lacks precision; as long as we keep north, we'll be all right. It was then that they interrupted my ploughing and set the egrets flapping.

Finding nothing up north, zigzagging from farmhouse to farmhouse, they arced up against the face of the Karkloof Hills and returned over the lip of the valley to the city. Back at the station, they took a police van and, following Sally's directions, headed up into the gullies where they had sighted the ponds.

The first house was large and Victorian and hidden among towering gums at the end of a rutted dirt road. As Marais parked the van on a gravel driveway, a phalanx of Dobermans bounded around a trellis of wistaria and surrounded the van, barking. Marais hooted twice and an aproned maid appeared from the front door and shooed away the dogs, all of which complied without hesitation, loping up steps to a corner of the deep verandah where they flopped down into baskets and watched the proceedings from over the wicker brims.

When Marais was told that the owners were away, he showed the maid his police identification and asked permission to walk around the garden. A burglar, he lied, had been seen in the vicinity and he just wanted to check that the man wasn't hiding in the azaleas at the foot of the lawn. Wide-eyed, the maid consented and retreated to the kitchen.

Behind the house, the view was dramatic. Sally said it reminded her of a painting of Florence: a view of a city nestled in a hollow. In the foreground, she said, was a band of forest beyond which was suburbia and the pastel serration of steeples.

The fishpond turned out to be unexpectedly large. Obviously a sunken garden at one time, it was now filled with water that trickled from an urn held by a lichen-covered Pan figure half-hidden in ferns. Under the lily pads idled schools of plump goldfish, their oranges and whites ribbed with sunlight. 'Look,' said Marais, pointing at the Pan, 'the clairvoyant woman said there was a statue near the pond.'

'So where's Alice?' asked Sally, squatting beside a flight of submerged steps and peering into the water, imagining a pale shape in the translucent greenness.

'Let's see,' said Marais, cutting a length of bamboo from a nearby copse. Thinking they were about to be fed, the fish shadowed him as he prodded the dark depths, periodically removing the stalk from the water and sniffing its tip for a whiff of putrefaction. Once he had circled the pond, prodding and sniffing, Sally said she repeated her question about Alice's whereabouts, this time with a hint of irony.

'I know where she is,' said Marais, pointing into the pond. 'There's a little bit of her in the belly of each goldfish.'

'No!' Sally said she exclaimed. 'How awful! How can you even think of things like that?"

'This isn't wonderland, you know,' said Marais pointedly. 'We are looking at the bottom of a pond. In case you've forgotten, people can't breathe down there. And fish are like goats. They eat anything.'

At that, Sally said, she withdrew momentarily, alarmed by Marais' coldness. Clearly, for him, the investigation was merely a job. If he wanted to find Alice at all, it was only because he feared the failure of not finding her. Whether it was an Alice or a Jill or even a Jack whom he sought, made little difference to him. But for Sally, it seemed, Alice had become almost a mythical symbol. She was Innocence personified, and her loss was a triumph for Evil. Only her safe-and-sound return could rebuff the powers of darkness.

The second pond was in a garden several miles further north. Retracing their tracks almost to suburbia, Sally and Marais edged up another rutted road through a pine plantation and into a tuggle of indigenous forest. At the very apex of the gully, in a wooded groin musical with the sound of streams in the undergrowth, they found stone gateposts and a driveway. Edging upwards between giant azaleas, they saw a large stone house encased in ivy. Near the front door was a young woman washing a cat. Kneeling beside a plastic tub, the woman was pouring water from a jug over a ginger tom that seemed misty-eyed with pleasure and was purring loudly.

'Hello,' said the woman, 'I'm Carol Lutwidge.'

'Hello,' said Marais. 'My name is Hannes Marais. I'm a detective. And this is Sally, my assistant. I'm sorry to bother you, but last night there was a burglary in a house down there behind those trees. We think the burglar may have come this way. May we just look around near your bottom fence to see if there are any footprints? If we find anything, we'll bring the dog squad.'

'Yes, sure,' said Carol Lutwidge. She was remarkably slight, said Sally, and wore hugging jeans and a checked shirt. 'Just shout if I can be of any help.'

Sally and Marais wandered down the lawn, pausing beside flowerbeds and peering for footprints in a masquerade of authenticity, before finding the pond beneath a spreading fig tree out of sight of the house. Marais peered beneath the lily pads and a layer of decomposing figs and saw several large Japanese koi circling slowly in the murkiness. Finding a broken branch, he sounded the depth and found it to be less than a metre.

'She's not here,' he said. 'It's so shallow we'd see her if she was. The bloody clairvoyants are talking rubbish again.'

'There could be another pond we haven't found,' said Sally.

'*Ja*,' said Marais, 'I suppose so.'

They then crossed the open lawn and walked along the perimeter fence enacting another dumb-show before returning to the house. Carol Lutwidge was seated with the cat on her lap, fluffing its coat with a hairdryer. Catching sight of them, she switched the dryer off and placed the tom on the ground beside her.

'Any luck?' she asked.

'Nothing,' said Marais.

'Does that mean the burglar didn't come through here?'

'Yes,' said Marais.

'Good,' said Carol. 'Come and have some tea.'

'Thank you,' said Marais although Sally told me later that she was anxious about being away from the paper so long.

Carol Lutwidge led the way through a large hall and down a passage to the kitchen where she switched on a kettle and emptied a mound of rock cakes from a baking tin onto a plate. Once the tea was made, they settled themselves in faded armchairs. Carol, Sally noticed, was so petite that her feet only touched the carpet when she leant forward to pour the tea. When she sat back on the sofa, her legs dangled like those of a child in a highchair.

Along the lower walls of the room were bookcases filled with an incongruous mix of militaria and cookery books, many of which, Sally said, were upside-down. Above them was a series of wildlife illustrations – elephants, lions and buffalo etched in black on copper backgrounds – and an array of plaques commemorating various operational zones in the Rhodesian bush war: Thraser, Repulse, Hurricane and Grapple. Marais asked about the plaques and Carol explained that her husband had been a helicopter pilot with the Rhodesian forces for several years.

The cat, Sally remembered, climbed onto Carol's lap and began preening itself, periodically pausing to smirk at no-one in particular. 'We must be leaving,' said Sally at the sound of a car outside.

'It'll be Charles,' said Carol, pushing the tom from her lap and dashing down the passage to the hall. After cries and laughter off-stage, she reappeared with her husband.

'This is Detective Marais and his assistant, Sally,' said Carol. 'They thought there was a thief in the garden but there isn't.'

'Jolly good,' said Charles, a boyish man with a ruddy face topped by a misshapen bush hat bristling with trout flies. 'You're not a nurse, I hope,' he said to Sally.

'No,' she replied.

'Good,' said Charles. 'So what's the difference between a nurse and a Cadillac?'

'I don't know,' they all replied.

'Not every man's been in a Cadillac.' At this Charles roared with laughter, shadow-boxing Carol who went into a defensive crouch and then pretended to punch him in the groin.

'Charles has been up in Zambia on business,' said Carol, discarding her mimicry.

'Oh,' Marais replied. 'What do you do?'

'Everything,' said Charles expansively, spreading his arms.

'We really must go,' Sally said she interjected.

'All the best.' said Charles. 'Give those criminals everything you've got. Otherwise they'll take it.' He exploded into laughter before looking at Sally with an expression of deep solemnity and patting her gently on the bottom. ''Bye Sally,' he said.

Back at the paper, Sally wrote a short story about a fruitless police search for Alice along the northern periphery of the city. Making no mention of clairvoyants and quoting an anonymous police source, she added that a breakthrough in the Alice mystery was expected soon. If there was no good news, she told me that evening, she and Marais had decided to manufacture some.

'You never know,' she said during supper. 'We may flush the abductor with a fib.'

10

I found it on the shelf among her underwear – a black notebook filled with scribbles. Forgetting the torch I was searching for, I violated her privacy and started picking through the pages. And so began – from my side at least – the first real deception of our relationship, Sally secretly writing her notebook and me secretly reading it.

Much of what Sally had written concerned Alice, but there were also reflections on our future as white South Africans, undigested snippets of philosophy, and a miscellany of observations. Both my good and bad points were chronicled, as well as Will's and Sergeant Marais'.

In several entries, Sally empathised with the Walkers, wondering what she would do if she had a daughter who disappeared. She would go public, of course, as Margaret had, if the police made no headway. But would she ever contemplate suicide during those low moments when she could see her daughter abused and then dispatched? No, she decided after much thought, because what if you were wrong and your child returned to find you dead because of her? As in *Romeo and Juliet*, such impetuosity often leads to greater tragedy. It was better, she concluded, to soldier on, putting a brave face on it and convincing yourself that if your child was dead, she was at peace – something the living have still to achieve.

The first entry, written shortly after our return from Kenya, captured well our ambivalence about the future:

Apartheid is dying, thank God, but now what? What retribution lies in wait for those of us whose forebears chose the southern tip of Africa and who now have no other home? Will we be dispossessed as we dispossessed others? Will we lose representation in the decision-making bodies as we deprived others of such representation? Will we be stigmatised because of our skin colour as we stigmatised others for theirs?

It's all very well for the new leaders to preach equality and reconciliation, but the wrongs of the past won't be so easily forgotten. Those who were downtrodden will want tangible proof of their newfound power. What benefit is there to be had for being in the driving seat if there are no rewards? And from where do the rewards come? From Chris and me and others of our kind? Will my future as a reporter on the Natal Times *be jeopardised by all the have-not journalists waiting in the wings? Journalists no more skilled than I, mind you, but ones awaiting long-promised positions?*

Will these five hundred acres that Chris farms so well be expropriated and divided among our labourers? After all, didn't their sweat also go into nurturing the herd of sleek cattle which now produces hundreds of thousands of litres of milk annually? The answer is deceptively simple: let the people cut up the farm into plots and have several cattle each for their own consumption. If they have more than they need, let them sell the surplus to their neighbours. In this paradise, everyone will be happy. While the country may go bankrupt, the people will experience the peace which was once theirs before the unwelcome arrival of whites from across the sea.

Other entries were less tinged with irony. For example: *Why won't Chris agree to emigrate when he admits we have no future here?*

And: *If Will must die soon, let him go suddenly in the dairy with Chris and the cows beside him, the milking machine running and the Karkloof Hills watching from a distance. Please don't let him go slowly, gasping in a hospital bed surrounded by oxygen cylinders.*

Dragging myself away, I pushed the notebook back among the bras and panties and the single black suspender belt that Sally wears on our occasional nights of horseplay.

Back in the sitting-room, I found her asleep in her chair with a voice on the radio reading the nine o' clock news. Moving through to the kitchen and making our customary nightcap of tea, I returned with two mugs as the newsreader announced the murder of a British holidaymaker on Lamu Island, off Kenya's coast. Nudging Sally awake, we sat and listened as the reader continued. Found at Shela Beach, the youth appeared to have bled to death from deep panga wounds to his head. Police had sealed off the beach and were searching the area for his killers.

And so, only months after we had seen that couple racing ecstatically to their climax among the dunes at Shela, a young man is hacked to death there with a panga. So much for our notion of an African paradise. The timelessness of those beaches, the coral walls, palms, dhows, the devotions of Islam and the image of a hybrid people lost in contentment was the illusion we should have known it was. Paradise is not only a location. It is a time as well. As I had confirmed for me shortly afterwards, a place can be paradise one second and hell the next.

11

One evening in early spring our next-door neighbour was murdered. Seventy-year-old Edward Mortimer was taking a bath at dusk when intruders burst through the door and cleaved his skull almost in two with a single blow of a panga. When the maid found him the following morning, she came straight to us. Sally had already left for work and I was ambling to the workshop when I heard screams from across the paddocks. No sooner had she told me the news than I grabbed a revolver from the house and, with Punch and Judy bounding beside me, sprinted towards the thatched roof that was just visible above the pinkness of cherry blossoms in the orchard.

Two messy contacts as a conscript in Angola hadn't prepared me for the awfulness of what I found. Having slid into the bath, Mortimer was half-submerged in brown water. Instinctively, I pulled the plug and watched as the muck drained and his frail, wrinkled body emerged. Despite its disfigurement, his face looked peaceful. Death, the district surgeon told me later, must have been instantaneous; he wouldn't have known what had happened to him.

'Have you checked the house?' I asked the maid in Zulu.

'There is no-one,' she replied.

Instructing her not to touch the door handle, I crossed to the phone in the hall. The wire had been cut. I then left the maid on guard and ran back to our house to phone the police. Returning to the Mortimers, I half-closed the bathroom door with my foot while the maid hovered beside me.

'When's the missus coming back?' I asked, knowing that Mary Mortimer was away, attending the birth of a grandchild.

'Next week,' said the maid in Zulu, exhaling in a sob before composing herself again.

'Was anything stolen?' I asked.

'The *umnumzana's* radio, and the box in his cupboard is open.'

56

'Show me the box,' I said.

The maid led me to the bedroom and opened the cupboard door. Behind a rack of suits was a gun safe, its door open and a key still in the lock. There were no firearms inside but sheaves of documents and a box of jewellery appeared untouched.

'What guns did the *umnumzana* have?' I asked.

'I don't know,' replied the maid.

At that point a yellow police van gunned up the driveway and three young constables – two whites and a black – sprang from the cab. I met them at the door. 'There,' I said, pointing to the bathroom.

'Jesus!' exclaimed the first policeman as he entered the room.

'Look,' said the other policeman who had walked around the lavatory. 'Here's the panga.'

'Jesus,' said the first policeman again, peering at the bits of bloody residue that clung to the blade. 'It looks bad.'

'What's the maid say?' asked the second policeman.

'Nothing much,' I said. 'It happened last night when she was off. It looks like a radio and some firearms were stolen.'

'Have a chat to her, Henry,' said the second policeman to his black associate.

'Fucking guns,' said the first policeman. 'Always fucking guns.'

At that point a car with Hannes Marais and another detective arrived. As they entered the bathroom I began to feel queasy. 'Can I go and sit outside?' I asked Hannes. 'I'm not feeling so good.'

'Yes,' he said. 'Get some fresh air.'

I crossed the lawn to a flatcrown and sat down in its shade. Several hadedahs picked their way along the drive, pecking at insects in the grass. Swallowtails flapped from flower to flower. Cattle lowed in our paddock beyond the cherry orchard. It was, I realised, a moment of momentous paradox: paradise outside and hell only metres away, within the spattered confines of the bathroom.

During the half-hour in which I sat under the flatcrown, the police worked hard, capturing sets of fingerprints on the edge of the basin, convinced of their veracity because of the smudges of blood incorporated in the tracery. Then the detectives summoned the Mortimers' employees. Once the maid and eight labourers were assembled on the lawn, the black constable began his interrogation.

What did they know of last night's happenings? Had they seen any strangers in the district? Did they know of anyone who had been speaking negatively of Mortimer? Looking exaggeratedly sombre, the employees shook their heads at every question. 'You mustn't lie,' said the black policeman. 'We can tell who did it from the fingerprints we got inside.'

'Fucking liars,' said the first policeman.

'And we'll get the dogs,' continued the black policeman. 'They know who did it.'

Realising that the interrogation was fruitless, the constable took down the employees' names and let them go. As the little group receded into the pinkness of the cherry blossoms, the two white constables emerged from the house, each carrying an end of a body bag containing Edward Mortimer's corpse. It is strange, I thought, as I watched the policemen dump the bag into their van, that sealed in that plastic bag is the man whom I had seen only yesterday pruning his roses in the little clearing below the orchard. Minutes later Hannes Marais and his companion emerged. Seeing me, Hannes crossed to the flatcrown, a camera in hand.

'Howsit going?' he asked.

'All right,' I replied.

'Do you know who's the old man's next of kin?'

'His wife,' I replied. 'She's staying with her daughter in Cape Town. Sally knows how to get hold of her.'

'Thanks,' he said. 'Are you going to push off now?'

'Yes,' I said. 'My men are working on the lands. I must go and check on them.'

'Cheers then,' said Marais. 'I'll be seeing you.'

'Any news of Alice Walker?' I asked.

'Not a whistle,' he said, shaking his head and getting into his van.

Calling Punch and Judy, I walked home via the cherry trees and paddocks. Unsure whether or not to phone Sally, I dithered briefly before deciding against it, knowing that Marais would tell her soon enough. I then set off past the dairy to the rye grass fields where the labourers were laying irrigation pipes. 'Everything all right?' I asked the *induna* and his three subordinates in Zulu as they adjusted sprinklers and coupled lengths of aluminium pipe together.

'Yes,' replied the *induna*.

'You heard about *baas* Mortimer?' I asked.

'Yes,' the four men replied.

'Very bad,' said the *induna* in Zulu.

'Yes,' said the other labourers. 'Sorry *nkosana*.'

As often before, I was struck by their dignified but unnecessary contriteness. Edward Mortimer was really nothing to them or to me, yet they commiserated with me because one of my kind had been killed.

'Yes, thank you,' I said. 'It is very bad.'

No sooner had I arrived back at the house than the phone rang. It was Sally. 'Hannes has just told me about Edward Mortimer. How awful! He says you found him?'

'Yes,' I said. 'Their maid called me.'

'Was he still alive?'

'No,' I said. 'Very dead.'

'I'm coming with a photographer,' Sally continued. 'Hannes is going to take us around. I'll see you later.'

Not knowing what to do with myself, and not feeling like eating any lunch, I sat on the verandah and gazed out across the fields. Dust above the cherry trees and the barking of a dog signified activity at the Mortimers' homestead but I didn't have the stomach to return there. Mid-afternoon Sally appeared briefly with a photographer and asked me more questions before rushing back to the newsroom to write her story.

The dog, apparently, found nothing. Primed in the bathroom, it headed straight for the maid's quarters not far from the back of the house. A question begged an answer: was the Doberman following the killer's scent or the maid's, or both? The police weren't sure, but they searched the maid's room and found nothing incriminating.

'I don't think she did it,' Marais told Sally, 'but she probably knows who did.'

Will returned from town at dusk. As he and Edward Mortimer had been good friends, Sally and I broke the news to him gently. Surprisingly, I thought, he took it badly, weeping briefly and wheezing for breath. Only after I had reassured him with platitudes about the need for a wide perspective to understand such things and Sally had poured him a brandy, did he regain his composure. Then we sat and watched the early television news, in which the murder got a brief mention, before talking about happier subjects as a counterpoint to the day's tragedy. After supper and a succession of brandies, Will began to flag, muttering inanities about Kenya and bloodshed between interludes of dozing.

'Would you like to sleep here tonight, Dad?' Sally asked.

'No thanks, my girl,' he replied, composing himself briefly. 'I'll take a pill and feel better in the morning.'

Needing assurance that the coast was clear, I called Punch and Judy before helping Will across the lawn to his cottage. Despite his insistence that he could manage, I helped him to bed and locked the front door behind me. The moon was full and heavy and its light sheened the corrugated-iron roofs of the dairy and calf pens. From a kraal in the valley beyond the rye grass fields came the sound of singing and the steady thump of tom-toms. Closer, in the darkness of the orchard, I knew the duikers would be busy, nosing delicately in the kikuyu grass for fallen fruit. Inside, Sally was bathing and through the open door I could see her graceful body half-lost in suds – the same view, I told myself, that the intruder would have had of Mortimer had the bathroom door been open.

'Does Hannes have any idea who did it?' I asked.

'He thinks it's probably a gang of outsiders looking for guns. He says they hear through the grapevine and then go for the softest targets. I suppose it'll be our turn next.'

'No,' I said, 'we're not soft enough.' Only half-believing myself, I turned on the taps and climbed into the shower. Thrusting my face towards the rose, I let the water pummel me for several minutes before I began washing.

12

Edward Mortimer's murder marked a watershed in the security arrangements in our district. Before this, the landowners had been singularly lax, ignoring attempts by the local army commando to form us into defensive cells linked by two-way radios. Unable to appreciate the extent of the lawlessness throughout the country, we retained the nonchalance of our parents and grandparents. This meant not bothering to have burglar guards fitted to every window, leaving the French doors ajar on summer evenings, taking siestas on the verandah or in a hammock in the garden, and even giving the Zulu maid a key so she could let herself into the kitchen first thing each morning.

While stock theft had increased, it never threatened our personal safety. Although legally entitled to shoot rustlers caught red-handed, we couldn't stop the stealing without electrifying all the fences and standing guard each night. Usually, the rustlers were long gone by the time a stock count didn't tally. Most farmers were convinced that none of their own labourers were involved, living under the misapprehension that one's own work force wouldn't dare bite the hand that feeds it. And so the disappearance of an occasional beast was tolerated, its loss worked into the farm's expenses.

Only after Edward's murder, however, did we sit up and take notice. With the veneer of peacefulness ruptured, we began to heed the commando's warnings, buying two-way radios and forming ourselves into cells for our mutual protection. We also began to ensure that windows were burglar-guarded, and double-checked that exterior doors were locked each night. We even deprived our maids of their kitchen key, instructing them instead to tap on the bedroom window early each morning so they could have the door unlocked for them.

Many families added to their pets, buying fox terriers to trigger the alarm and Dobermans and bull mastiffs for muscular backup.

Some landowners bought geese which honked whenever a stranger approached the house. Other farmers, among them several Indian families who had bought land in the district after the repeal of the Group Areas Act, even had their homesteads enclosed by an electric fence which they switched on each night.

Nevertheless the violence continued. Almost daily, the press carried accounts of gruesome killings. Edward Mortimer's was no exception. Sally and the photographer did a six-column spread of reportage with a mugshot of Mortimer beside views of the murder scene. Elderly people living on farms had become the principal targets: couples knifed in their beds, or gunned down while opening a gate. Like most people, Sally and I were soon benumbed by the media's litany of death – seeing, hearing or reading, then forgetting. But insidiously the cumulative effect was mounting. Stress rocketed. Alcohol flowed. Marriages crumbled. Some homes were imploded by family murders. The threat of violence became the norm.

Suburban homeowners also began to take greater precautions, installing burglar alarms and panic buttons and heat-sensitive exterior lights. Even the Walkers had a security company assess their defences. On a morning that Sally was paying Margaret Walker one of her regular supportive visits, the owner of a local security company was instructing Duncan to replan his garden for safety reasons.

'Where are your main points of entry?' asked the man in mock-military uniform and dark glasses with a revolver at his hip.

'I suppose the driveway and that archway covered with roses,' said Duncan Walker, pointing across the garden.

'Good, good,' said the paramilitary. 'Both clear. But see that hedge. It must go. The enemy can use it for cover.'

'I don't think my wife will be too pleased,' said Duncan, looking up at Margaret and Sally on the verandah.

'Hey,' said the paramilitary, 'this is not a time to cry about flowers. Otherwise you may lose another daughter.' And he laughed.

'No,' said Duncan.

'See that trellis there,' the man continued, pointing at a cascade of jasmine near Alice's bedroom window.

'Yes,' said Duncan.

'That's good, very good,' said the man. 'It doesn't block your fire and it will deflect grenades.'

And so the defence lesson continued. Riding roughshod over the Walkers' and Sally's sensibilities, the paramilitary soon made the house impregnable to an armed assault.

'I must be going now,' he said at last. 'I'll send you a quote. Don't have too many sleepless nights until I sort things out.'

'Goodbye,' said Duncan.

The man strode down the path and clanged the gate behind him, causing the roses on the archway to tremble.

'Bloody Rambo,' said Duncan Walker. Then he too left, reversing from the garage into Gatacre Drive.

'Duncan's started drinking heavily,' Margaret said to Sally. 'He doesn't watch TV anymore. He just sits by himself in his study and finishes almost a bottle of gin every night. Sometimes he listens to the radio or puts on a tape, but mostly he just sits and drinks. Whenever I go in and see him he says nothing. He just wants to be by himself.'

'Does he ever talk about Alice?' asked Sally.

'Sometimes,' said Margaret. 'I'm sure he thinks about her all the time. Like I do.'

Exaggerating the progress made by the police, Sally painted her usual reassuring picture of the investigations. Concealing the fact that several possible grave sites were being excavated around Bushmansburg, she made much of the sighting in Cape Town of a girl who fitted Alice's description. 'I've got a hunch that girl's Alice,' said Sally. 'It won't be long before the police pick her up.'

'But why doesn't she come home by herself?' asked Margaret.

'I don't know,' said Sally. 'Perhaps she's confused.'

Doris brought tea and sandwiches and the two women sat eating and drinking on the verandah. When they had finished, Margaret took Sally to see Alice's bedroom. Although she had glimpsed it during her first visit nine months previously, Sally said she was strangely affected by the pink bower with its posters of Tom Cruise and George Michael. Like the stock photograph of Alice used by the press, it endorsed Sally's impression of a child on the threshold of womanhood. Not quite a Lolita, but certainly a girl in bobby socks with an eye for the boys.

'I can see her back here,' said Sally. 'She is reading on the bed and the radio is playing.'

'Dear God,' said Margaret.

As they neared the car with its red *Natal Times* logo, Margaret said hesitantly: 'I'm going to the spiritualist church on Sunday. If Alice is no longer with us, she may have a message. Sally, will you come with me?'

'Yes,' said Sally.

13

I have seen people throw their television sets from the second floor, or push their furniture into the middle of the road and soak it in petrol and burn it. Children are smashing their toys with hammers on the pavements.

This quote headed the next entry in Sally's diary. Taken from a *Natal Times* article commemorating the 30th anniversary of France's withdrawal from Algeria, and written by a young officer who witnessed the colonists abandon the city of Oran, it was an apocalyptic fragment that had clearly got Sally thinking. She continued:

Will we too have to withdraw? If we do, will our withdrawal be as bitter? Will Chris take a hammer to the milking machine and douse the tractors in diesel before setting them alight? Will he herd the milkers and calves into the night paddocks near the house and shoot them one by one with his army rifle? Once they are all dead, will he open their guts with a chainsaw and pour in rat poison to ensure that no-one can eat them? Will I make a pyre of bedspreads and curtains on the lawn? As we leave, with our truck filled with a few possessions and Chris riding shotgun while I drive, will we see our house go up in flames and across the hills see other homes burning as our neighbours join the great retreat?

Why doesn't Chris think of this possibility? As negotiations break down, why isn't he traumatised by the sense of impending loss? Is he being strong or weak? For him life is peacefulness and cattle and the pleasure of rye grass growing green during winter. To him I am merely his best friend whom he kisses or bonks when he wants to. We've been together six years and I still don't understand. Doesn't he grasp what's happening, or does he just keep it all bottled up? Can't he see the collapse? Alice Walker's disappearance and Edward Mortimer's murder should be proof enough. But he just plods on like an ox to the slaughter.

In writing that, Sally did me a disservice. But not being able to challenge her without blowing my cover, as it were, I had to leave things as they were. I considered acting differently to reassure her. It wouldn't have been honest, of course, but it would have served a purpose. If my ploy had worked, she should have been pleased with my transformation. Her diary among her underwear could have become a barometer of how my efforts were being received. Like the producer of a soap opera, I could have looked to my audience for guidance.

But the Algerian parallel is an apt one. As you have seen, fear and violence are part of life in South Africa. And the possibility of a scorched-earth exodus by whites and Indians remains their worst scenario. So let's take Sally's agitated musings further, contriving a doomsday vision of what could happen:

Assuming Will is dead (our imagined flight being too harrowing for someone of his frailty), we leave Punch and Judy to fend for themselves and gun the truck down the drive as the fire in the sheds finds the petrol drums and flames rocket above the pines. Refugees are converging on the district road, forming a bizarre convoy of Mercedes' and Toyotas interspersed with trucks and tractors towing trailers piled high with possessions. Most of the drivers are women with their men as armed guards, either in the passenger seat with a rifle or shotgun protruding from the open window, or perched high on the backs of trucks, camouflaged in piles of blankets or crouching behind pieces of furniture. On one trailer a Jersey bull, presumably some priceless import, is guy-roped among tiers of tea chests and several cats in baskets.

Black figures, all running, cross the pastures and mealie fields, either heading for the abandoned homes or staging sudden forays at weak points in the convoy. Shots ring out, figures fall and the panga-wielding gangs withdraw into adjoining wattle plantations where they consolidate for their next attack. On the national road linking the hinterland with the sea, the line of vehicles stretches to the horizon. Forcing our way into the procession, we snail towards the Bushmansburg bypass like everyone else headed for Durban's airport or harbour. Desperation and kinship characterise the demeanour of the refugees: everyone for himself but each aware of what will happen to those left behind.

With some safety in numbers, we reach the edge of the escarpment above Bushmansburg and descend into the valley. Smoke billows from the residential areas and explosions shatter factories, slinging glass shards towards the highway. In places, the tarmac has melted and the tyres of the vehicles churn the surface into a glutinous sludge.

Marauding gangs are everywhere, firing shots and throwing stones and petrol bombs from the roadside or attacking vehicles containing only women or old people, but accurate covering fire keeps them at bay. Some cars are overrun and left to their fate. On vacant land beside the highway, a platoon of soldiers fights its way towards a flyover from which black youths are dropping rocks onto the fleeing cars. A Porsche two ahead of us has its windscreen shattered and veers onto the verge. Leaping from the back of a lorry, a burly youth sprints across the tarmac to the stricken car, pulling its bleeding driver from the cab and lugging him back to the convoy seconds before a raiding party appears. We are lucky. Under fire from the advancing troops, the youths seek cover as we pass beneath them.

Hereafter, bridges become our nightmare. Wherever the police or troops have pickets, we are safe, but en route to Durban many of the flyovers are undefended and we entrust our lives to fate and press on, thanking God or whoever when the vehicle in front of us is hit and slews sideways, allowing us time to get through before the next rock is dropped.

Sally is marvellous, weaving the truck between barricades of wreckage as I fire out of the passenger window. Unusually perhaps, I try not to kill anyone, keeping to my semi-pacifist code as I did as a conscript during harrowing advances deep into Angola. Maiming, not killing, was my intention. I even winged a Cuban once, but he didn't die. Having survived that ordeal without a death on my hands, I am determined to keep my slate clean. Why? Because of a loathing to end life or as foolhardy protection against some future retribution? Who knows? Consequently, scooping bullets from a pile in the footwell, I fill my magazine and aim carefully for the attackers' extremities, adhering to the maxim of minimum force and blowing limbs to pieces in preference to heads and torsos.

By some fluke we reach Durban. At the sight of the sea after miles of invisibility from the smoke of cane fires, a loud hurrah goes up from the convoy. Crazed by now, some of the passengers fire salvoes into the air. As we enter the suburbs, we see a roadblock manned by police and soldiers and backed by heavily-armoured vehicles. They wave us through and we snake into the city itself, harried only by sporadic sniper fire.

Among many others, Sally and I head for the British Consulate. Whites and Indians are running helter-skelter in the streets and Land Rovers filled with soldiers comb the alleys for blacks. Shots ring out from the city hall and among the palms in the adjoining gardens mounds of black corpses mark the sites of summary executions. With the invincibility of the desperate we force our way into the consulate and demand repatriation.

'What claim do you have to British protection?' asks the official behind the counter.

'We're English,' I say, 'but our families have been in Africa for five generations.'

The official is unimpressed, shaking his head in a charade of sympathy. 'We are closing down today,' he says. 'British Airways will be flying British nationals out from this afternoon. I'm sorry, but your only hope is the Red Cross planes. They're due in tomorrow.'

'But look at us,' Sally enunciates, her voice tremulous with emotion. 'Listen to the way we speak. Can't you see we're English?'

'No,' says the official with an eerie calm. 'You may look English. You may sound English. But you're not English.'

'Well, fuck you!' shrills Sally.

We dash back to the truck and gun for the harbour. As we near the stevedore sheds, firing can be heard from the suburbs where the perimeter troops are covering our retreat. Accelerating beneath rows of cranes, we pass a crowd of refugees and head for the end of the quay. There, beyond the dry dock, we find a rusting tanker with a Greek flag suspended from its stern.

'Where's the captain?' I shout at a sailor on the deck.

Presently a portly man appears. 'What do you want?' he enquires in heavily-accented English. I put our case: passage to Europe for Sally and me with our truck and possessions.

'You got no papers,' says the captain. 'The police. They will make trouble.'

'For Christ's sake,' I retort. 'There's no law and order anymore. Can't you hear the gunshots?'

'There is fighting, yes,' says the captain.

'Let me show you something,' I continue.

Cautiously, with the sailor beside him, the captain beckons us up the gangplank. 'Look,' I say, turning my back on the sailor and unwrapping a parcel to reveal a gold dagger encrusted with emeralds. 'It comes from India. You can see it's very valuable. Get us out of Africa and you can have it.'

'But we must get to Greece,' adds Sally. 'There must be no trouble. I am a journalist and our friends know we are on your boat. Only when we get to Athens will we give you the knife.'

'All right,' says the captain.

The dagger, it seems, has done the trick. Part of my grandfather's imperial booty, it has secured our escape as the last outpost falls. Within half an hour the truck is on deck, encased in a tarpaulin. As we weigh anchor and edge past the emptying berths, a group of refugees finds our quay and their cries recede as we head for the harbour mouth.

It is dusk when we reach the open sea and, as the sky darkens, so the glows of cane fires begin to extend along the coastline. On we plough through the night, past Zululand and towards Mozambique. Sally and I huddle in our cabin like children, alternately appalled and delighted by what has happened.

For several days we head northwards, skirting the Comores and Zanzibar before entering Kenyan waters. On nearing Mombasa, Sally and I peer into the haze, hoping to see the Leonards' house, but can't find it in the heat. Then Lamu appears as a dot in the distance and we remember the lesson learned there: that hell and paradise are intertwined.

Next comes Somalia, with its anarchy and starving millions, before we round the horn and head for Suez. As Europe nears, so we feel a bittersweet lightening of spirit. It's goodbye to Africa and hello to ....

Short of being killed, that scorched-earth exodus is the worst scenario – a hell, it is hoped, that will get no further than Sally's notebook. Either way, it doesn't involve me directly. I'm out of it now, as you'll soon discover.

14

The following Sunday, Sally collected Margaret and drove to the spiritualist church. One of several red-brick Victorian cottages in a side-street near Bushmansberg station, it had clearly seen better days. An ugly portico had been added to its facade and the paint on its corrugated-iron roof was peeling. The street itself had also changed. The sterile neatness of an exclusively white residential area had succumbed to the vibrant shabbiness of multi-racial homes and businesses. On a low wall where a few years previously only sleek cats had preened themselves, several black street-children were shouting and whistling. In short, said Sally, it was one of those areas where Africa couldn't be held at bay any longer. Because of this, most of the whites who could afford it had cut their losses and retreated.

Taking a pew at the back, Sally and Margaret waited while white matrons who all seemed to know each other filed into the church. Notable among the few men present were two young blacks in ties and blazers. Otherwise the congregation was exclusively white, mostly female and elderly. Sally said Margaret was clearly nervous, repeatedly dabbing her brow with a handkerchief. When Sally turned to her, she smiled weakly and looked away, pretending to read the article on spiritualism by Arthur Conan Doyle at the front of her hymnbook.

Once everyone was seated, one of the matrons left the front pew and made her way slowly to the lectern. After a brief introduction, she announced that anyone wanting to communicate with the spirit world should hand a personal item – like a watch, ring or key-ring – to a young woman seated on the stage. Sally declined but Margaret handed in her wedding ring.

The matron then led the service of hymns, prayers and a recitation of the seven principles of spiritualism. Midway through the service, she called on a middle-aged man sitting at the back of the stage to deliver the lesson. Sally said he had a large, Kitchener-type moustache. He strode to the lectern and said a few introductory words in a soft voice. He seemed diffident at first. Then, closing his eyes and lifting his face, he began a strange, resonant, sonorous address, sweeping his arms in wide gestures and on one occasion almost knocking over a flower arrangement.

The thrust of his lesson was a warning against the demons of drink, drugs and licentiousness but what struck Sally more than the hackneyed content was his comically portentous delivery. From time to time, she said, he would pause and pronounce a word slowly, breaking it up into syllables and explaining with an eerie radiance that several invisible guides on the stage beside him were speaking through him. He spoke for about twenty minutes. In his conclusion, he carried out what appeared to be a ritual extending of his arms and then bending them horizontally in front of himself while he mumbled several parting words. Sally watched as he paused and his face broke out into a radiant smile. He then opened his eyes and, speaking normally, thanked the congregation for their attention before returning to his seat.

I have forgotten much of Sally's account of the service, but shortly after the lesson, the clairvoyant was called to centre stage. She was youngish and blonde and dressed in a pastel frock with flounces around the collar. Reaching the lectern, she placed the tray of personal items covered by a blue cloth on a table beside her and raised a gold watch in her hand.

'I feel very good about this,' she said in a little-girl voice. 'I see sun and laughter.' She clasped the watch in her hand and, closing her eyes, put it to her forehead. 'It's very beautiful,' she said.

'Thank you,' said someone from the audience.

Next, the clairvoyant raised a collection of keys. 'I see darkness here,' she said quietly. 'I see a ship on the mantelpiece and an axe. There is a cold wind. Someone in the spirit world is calling but I can't hear them clearly. You must be careful.'

No-one in the audience responded.

The clairvoyant then produced Margaret's wedding ring from under the cloth on the tray. She held it up for identification. Margaret nodded and the clairvoyant noted her presence by smiling briefly. 'I see lots of branches and doors,' she said. 'I have a feeling of falling. But there is an old woman. She is in the spirit world. I can see her in a wheelchair. She has a blanket over her knees. Her grey hair is tied back and she has a beautiful, kind face. She is saying "Maggie, don't worry." But there are lots of branches and running and doors slamming. And there is sadness.'

Margaret nodded and the clairvoyant smiled in acknowledgement. Then the next item emerged from under the cloth and the communication moved on.

'God,' said Margaret under her breath, placing a hand on the pew beside Sally, 'that was my mother.'

Once the clairvoyance was over, a final hymn was sung and a prayer recited. Then the congregation handed in their hymnbooks, collected their objects from the clairvoyant's tray and filed out into the street. The light was bright. Margaret and Sally hurried to the car. No sooner were they out of sight of the others than Margaret burst into tears. Sally placed an arm around her. 'It was awful,' said Margaret, between stifled sobs. 'All the branches and running and slamming doors. That must have been something about Alice.'

'But your mother said "don't worry",' said Sally, starting the car and edging into the street beneath the purple canopy of jacarandas. 'Being a spirit, she must know everything.'

'Don't worry about what?' asked Margaret, wiping her eyes with a handkerchief. 'Don't worry because Alice's all right or because she's dead and mother knows and doesn't want me to grieve if it's all over and there's nothing we can do about it?'

'I don't know,' said Sally. 'But she did say "don't worry" and she didn't say Alice is dead. If Alice is dead, the clairvoyant would have known. She knows about your mother. We must look at it positively. And we mustn't let ourselves worry.'

Margaret said little as Sally drove her home. From the city centre the road winds northwards, over a bridge and up into wooded suburbs with their large houses and neat gardens. Just beyond a tearoom, the road forks and Sally swung right, skirting the finger of indigenous bush and heading back towards Gatacre Drive, taking the route everyone wished Alice had chosen but travelling in the opposite direction. 'Lots of branches,' thought Sally, gazing at the mesh of trees and undergrowth.

When they reached the Walkers' home, Margaret invited Sally inside for tea. They sat in the sun-room with its Laura Ashley patterns and talked about the service. Doris brought in the tray and Sally poured the tea while Margaret went over the clairvoyant's message in desperate detail, hoping that some hidden pointer would emerge. At one stage she disappeared briefly and returned with a photograph of her mother. 'She's the old woman the clairvoyant was talking about,' Margaret said, handing the photograph to Sally.

'Yes,' said Sally, 'she does have a beautiful, kind face.'

'What do you think about the branches and running? And the falling and doors slamming?' Margaret asked.

'I don't know,' said Sally.

'God,' said Margaret, her voice tremulous, 'I don't know if it was a good thing to have gone to the service. It's just got me more worked up.'

'No,' said Sally. 'It doesn't have to be bad. When you think about it, nothing really negative was said. The clairvoyant did mention that there was sadness but that may have been our sadness because of Alice's disappearance and nothing to do with what may have happened to her.'

'I don't know,' said Margaret.

They sat in silence briefly, drinking tea and eating shortbread, before Sally spoke. 'Where's Duncan?' she asked.

'Probably sleeping,' said Margaret. 'The funny thing is he's always sleeping and I can't sleep. I take pills and they help a bit but I dread going to bed every night.' She paused. 'Under the sink in the kitchen we've got a bottle of caustic soda. Doris uses it to unblock the drains. Sometimes I tell myself when I can't sleep that I must go and drink it all so that it'll unblock my insomnia and I can sleep forever.'

'You shouldn't talk like that,' said Sally.

'I know,' said Margaret, 'but I can't help it.'

15

On the day after the church service, Sally did something very rash. She wrote an untrue story about the Alice Walker mystery. Although she had taken liberties with the truth before, this was the first time she had deliberately written lies.

All this I discovered several days later from her confessional notebook among the underwear in her cupboard. In sequence, this is what seems to have happened:

Affected by the sight of Alice's bedroom waiting neatly for her return and the medium's ambiguous message, Sally phoned Marais from the newspaper on the Monday morning and told him her plan. To quote from her confession:

I told Hannes that I can't bear Alice being lost any longer. Her parents are cracking up. The investigation is getting nowhere. I told him I'm going to pretend we have information we don't have. Maybe that will get things started again.

Marais was reluctant at first. But it seems that his infatuation with Sally was greater than I had suspected. Her argument was simple: with no progress made, they had nothing to lose.

She then wrote thirty centimetres of absolute fantasy. An anonymous source, she said, had reliably linked Alice Walker's disappearance to MAL, the Movement for Azanian Liberation. As is commonly known, MAL is a group of exclusively black radicals on the very left of the political spectrum. Whites are not eligible for membership. If they were, only the deranged would subscribe, knowing that MAL's intention is the eradication of everything European. 'One white, one bullet,' was their rallying call. Like the white heavies on the far right, who would think nothing of destroying the country to restore apartheid, MAL's militants would gladly do the same in the name of black purity.

Members of MAL, Sally wrote in her article, allegedly abducted

Alice from the finger of bush between Gatacre Drive and the neighbouring suburb. They then took her to a house in the black township of Edenvale, raped and killed her. Information had been received that random murders in white suburbia were part of MAL's new strategy. Fearful of an agreement between moderate political groupings, they were determined to polarise the races. 'White settler racist society,' said one of their communiqués, 'has to be completely destroyed before a new non-racist African culture can be born.' MAL spokesmen, Sally wrote, could not be reached for comment. And she concluded by saying that the police expected to make arrests soon.

Fearful that the news editor would hold her story for verification, Sally delayed submitting it until early evening. Once the day staff had left, she fed it through to the night sub-editors, giving the impression that it had the news editor's blessing. So much of a *cause celèbre* had the Alice Walker case become that the story was hard to restrain. Consequently, when confronted by a possible scoop, the night editor grasped it with both hands. During his routine phone call to the editor at nine o'clock, he motivated strongly that the story lead the front page. The editor was more cautious and phoned Sally at home before agreeing to publish it. We were watching television when the phone rang. I answered and called Sally. She spoke for several minutes and then returned to the sitting-room.

'Any problem?' I asked.

'No,' she said, 'there's been a bit of a breakthrough with Alice Walker. One of Hannes's sources has information. It looks like MAL had something to do with it. The editor was just checking my story.'

'Jesus,' I said, 'does Hannes think he's got it?'

'He's not sure,' she said. 'But it looks like it.'

'Why didn't you tell me?' I asked.

'I was just waiting for the phone call and then I was going to tell you,' she said. 'Now that they are going to use it, I can.' She smiled.

She then told me the story and I believed her completely. Only now does it seem strange that she said nothing before the phone call. She may have feared I would ask too many questions.

She had come home late and from reading her diary I now know she had dropped in at the Walkers and alerted Margaret to her ploy. It was just after dusk and Duncan was already drunk. That was the first time Sally had proof of his deterioration and it helped convince her that shock tactics were necessary. With her life disintegrating around her, Margaret took little persuading. As Duncan was beyond inclusion, she gave Sally her blessing, bracing herself for the following morning's revelation.

In her diary, Sally cited a British case in which the press and police had co-operated to catch a murderer. Several women had been raped and killed in London. Forensic tests indicated a single killer. Fibreglass was found on each corpse, suggesting the women had been murdered in the same place before being dumped in different parts of the Thames. Consequently, every registered fibre-glass business in London was investigated, but without success.

When all leads ran dead and all hope of solving the case seemed lost, the police turned to the newspapers. False stories were published. At first the articles stated that the police were following strong leads; then they intimated that further progress was being made. Finally, a story appeared announcing that a suspect was expected to be arrested within twenty-four hours.

The police then sat back and waited for the suicide reports. Each male was investigated. Among the dead was a bachelor canoeist. It turned out that he had met each woman at a singles bar, taken her home, and then raped and murdered her. He then placed each body in his canoe and transported it to the Thames on his roof-rack during his early-morning training sessions. The murders ceased and the case was closed.

Sally said MAL would inevitably deny the accusation but as the reward for information about Alice had been increased to fifty thousand rand, the reverberations could well revive the case.

Our breakfast the next morning was peculiar. Assuming Sally would want to leave for work earlier than usual, I left the labourers to complete the milking and returned to the house. The paper had arrived and Sally was in the sitting-room reading it. I crossed to the sofa and stood behind her. The story was above the fold on the front page. It's bold heading read: *MAL killed Alice Walker – claim.* Sally's byline was in large type. As I read it, I ran my fingers through her hair.

'God,' I said when I had finished, 'how terrible! Do Margaret and Duncan Walker know?'

'I phoned them,' said Sally. 'They're very upset, but they'll be alright. It's better that the case is closed one way or another.'

Throughout the meal, Sally was strangely animated. Assuming her excitement to be delight at the breakthrough, I was almost archly supportive. My talk was full of compliments and not once did I question the origins of the article.

No sooner had Sally left than the phone began to ring. 'I know nothing more than's in the article,' was my stock response, and I deflected each caller to Sally at the paper.

When she reached her desk, Sally said later, she found a mound of message slips. The phone had been been going mad. Fellow journalists crossed to her cubicle to offer congratulations. Sifting through the names and numbers, Sally found a message from Margaret Walker and phoned her immediately. Let me embellish her diary entry:

Margaret was confused and slightly hysterical. 'I've told Duncan,' she shrilled. 'He's a bit hung over but he understands. He's going to stay at home today. It'll look good and he won't have to answer too many questions. But my friends have been going mad with support. Three have visited already. It's hard pretending to be totally devastated when you're only partly so. Doris is beside herself. I've sent her to her room. And the other papers have been pestering me for the last hour. They want interviews but I have refused. Each time I tell them I only deal with you.'

'Phone your doctor,' said Sally, 'and get him to give you a strong sedative. It'll make you feel so switched-off that you won't have to pretend. And get a friend to answer the phone and say that neither you nor Duncan can talk to anyone.'

Sally then began responding to all the messages, hoping that one would provide the crucial lead. As she did so, she thought of Alice imprisoned somewhere, oblivious of the furore her death had caused. It occurred to her again that Alice may really have absconded voluntarily but she brushed the thought aside. Anyway, she assured herself, no minor is allowed to run away. She must be found whether she wants to be or not.

Without exception, the callers wanted to express their outrage and sorrow at the fact and manner of Alice's death. While the majority were whites, many Indians, Coloureds and blacks were also sufficiently appalled to respond. All saw the defilement and murder of a beautiful young woman as a crime against humanity.

According to the callers, even deep political wounds were insufficient excuse for this brutal crime. Many demanded revenge and responses were often studded with expletives. The more restrained called for MAL to be banned, feeling that any organisation that failed to work towards a peaceful, democratic society should be declared illegal. The less restrained demanded a call to arms to give MAL some of their own medicine. The intolerant would not be tolerated, said one caller.

No-one questioned her sources, Sally noted with relief in her diary. The mere fact that it was published in a newspaper seemed sufficient proof of the story's authenticity.

Then the editor summoned Sally to his office. Let's imagine their dialogue:

'Who is your source?' he asked.

'As I told you last night, Mr White,' she said, 'I got it from the police.'

'Who in the police?'

'I'm sorry, I can't say.'

'But how do you know it isn't a pack of lies?' he asked.

'I just know,' she replied. 'You'll have to trust me.'

'So you wrote it in good faith and have no reason to believe it untrue?'

'Yes.'

'MAL is threatening legal action,' he continued. 'But we will have to sit tight for now and see what happens.'

'I'm sorry,' said Sally. 'I was just doing my job.'

16

The first bombshell came the next day. Sally and I were eating supper and watching television when the phone rang. I went through to the hall and lifted the receiver. It was Marais. Could he speak to Sally? I called her and returned to my food and the news. We made a habit of watching the eight o'clock bulletin every evening as Sally, being a journalist, felt an obligation to keep abreast of everything.

Five minutes later, Sally reappeared. Her face was ashen. 'Something terrible's happened,' she said, sitting down slowly on the edge of her chair. 'The police have found the body of a black man. He had been tortured and killed. Hannes says his killers used a soldering iron to burn '1 Alice, 10 kaffirs' on his chest. My article must have caused it.'

'Christ,' I said. Sally started crying. I moved to her and put my arm around her shoulders. 'It's not your fault, Sal,' I said. 'You were just reporting what happened.' But Sally was inconsolable. 'Things are out of control now,' I continued, seeking words of solace. 'Political loonies do what they like. You're just a reporter.'

Of course, at that stage, I was unaware of the true extent of Sally's predicament. But thanks to her diary, I soon knew more than I wanted to. From a certain perspective, the corpse was hers in both senses, if you see what I mean. She created the story and hence the killing. And the killing devastated her. In any case, it had to be partly her fault. But where does blameworthiness end? Even Alice was an unwitting accomplice. Had she not decided to go for a swim or whatever, nothing would have happened. Let's take it further. Blame the heat if she was hot. Blame adolescence if she wanted to tan to increase her attractiveness. Blame everything.

In fact, Sally had unwittingly committed a near-perfect crime. She had arranged the murder and had someone else do the deed for her. The victim was somewhat random, perhaps, but there is no disputing an ingenious set-up had she deliberately engineered it. But she hadn't.

Pushing her food aside, Sally hurried through to the bathroom and vomited into the lavatory. With her face moist and as pale as eggshell, she then ran a bath and lay deep in the water. I found a sedative in the medicine cabinet and gave it to her with a mug of black tea and more reassuring words.

Once she was tucked up in bed, I went through to the sitting-room to switch off the lights and lock the interleading doors. Since Edward Mortimer's murder all the farmers in the district had begun to entomb themselves behind a succession of locks before bed each night.

While I was jangling keys, it never once occurred to me that Sally might have been over-reacting. Stunted by my own self-control, I had come to respect visible emotion in others. As Sally had said in her diary, my passivity is exasperating. Little does she know of the turmoil behind my implacable facade; the urge for mayhem that so often rises in my gorge and is only just snuffed out in time.

After brushing my teeth and changing into my pyjamas, I switched off the passage light and felt my way through the darkness to our bed. The sedative must have been working because Sally was breathing deeply and regularly. I moved up against her and tried to sleep but couldn't expel the spectre of the mutilated youth. The white right has struck, I remember thinking with a strange mixture of dread and calm acceptance.

Sometime after midnight, I was woken by the two-way radio in the passage. Disorientated, I sat up in bed as an emergency message crackled through the static: 'Mayday! Mayday! This is Zulu 326, George Ferguson of Bushbuck Bend. House has been attacked. We're okay for now in the bedroom. Barns are burning and they're trying to break down the garage doors. Need support. Call the police. Over.'

Each of us belonged to a cell for which we were responsible, and Bushbuck Bend was too far away for me to respond. Neighbouring cells came to each other's aid, but because of the danger of conges-tion, distant members of the network remained merely on standby until called for. Another danger was deception: the diversionary assault to lure the husbands away so their wives and children could be attacked. So a delicate balance had to be struck between helping one's neighbour and protecting oneself.

A radio monitor near the Fergusons assumed control, co-ordinating the relief operation. Citing their call-signs or reaction-force numbers, farmers began to respond over the air as they rushed to pre-arranged rendezvous points before going in. I had learnt the drill by heart: two up in a truck, one driving while the passenger trains an army rifle on the darkness through the open window. The objective was simple: save your neighbour, ideally by supporting the police, but if they hadn't appeared, it was over to you. A fire-fight in the shrubbery, perhaps, or hot pursuit through the mealie fields. Although the orders stipulated only a defensive response, it was hard to remain temperate when your blood was up.

That night, the police responded promptly to the call. After an exchange of fire, the attackers fled into a wooded gully. Reluctant to follow without spotlights and dogs, the farmers and police congregated in a paddock and waited in the glare of the burning barn. Within minutes the Dobermanns arrived and the posse descended into the valley.

All this I picked up from the radio in the passage, the crackling dialogue tracing the sequence. As the first light of dawn began to appear through the curtains, I caught the denouement from the radio monitor: one attacker shot dead and four others arrested. And the Fergusons were safe.

How should I respond? I remember asking myself. With delight, sorrow or indifference? Confused and exhausted, I fell into bed beside Sally and caught a last hour of sleep before the sound of the milking machine dragged me awake.

17

The second bombshell came several days later. No sooner had I sneaked a look at Sally's diary and discovered her anguish, than another entry took my breath away. But first things first.

The morning after Marais' phone call about the youth's murder, Sally was understandably subdued. After a hurried but silent breakfast she left for work and I went about my usual chores – checking on the dipping of the cattle and driving to the agricultural co-op for calf pellets and fertiliser.

Early in the afternoon Sally phoned to say she was going with Marais to watch the state pathologist perform an autopsy on the youth. Beyond a slight puzzlement, I thought nothing of it. But when she hadn't returned by dark, I became worried. However, she phoned at seven to say she had forgotten a staff party – a few farewell drinks in the paper's library for a fellow journalist who was emigrating to Australia.

She finally returned at nine. I remember the time because the news was ending. 'Sorry I'm late,' she said, barely pausing in the sitting-room. 'I must have a bath.'

'How was the autopsy?' I asked.

'Horrible,' she said. 'I'll tell you later.'

She never did tell me in detail. But again, thanks to her diary, I've pieced it together.

She was reading in bed when I entered the room. I took the book from her gently and traced her shoulders lightly with my lips, inscribing little circles on her skin with the tip of my tongue. When it rippled with gooseflesh and the fine blonde hairs at the nape of her neck stirred, I licked them too. Then she shivered with what I took to be pleasure and I rolled her over gently and began to caress the smoothness of her breasts, moistening my index finger and rubbing its wetness onto her nipples. 'Sally,' I said, catching my breath. 'Let's do it.' With hindsight it seems an ordinary enough request: the familiar, almost leisurely option, so unlike our occasional mad couplings, of which Lamu's was the last.

'I can't,' she said. 'My period's started.'

'Oh Christ,' I said, hard and breathless.

'Don't blame me. Blame Mother Nature.'

Suppressing my disappointment, I kissed Sally again and we lay together in the dark until sleep came.

While shaving the next morning, I nicked myself and dabbed a piece of wet cotton wool to my chin as a bandage. Several minutes later, once the bleeding had stopped, I carefully removed the cotton wool and dropped it in a bin beside the lavatory. In the second that the lid was open, I noticed the bin was empty. While my observation may seem unremarkable in itself, it is a crucial point, as you will see.

I had to attend a farmers' meeting that night, so was away from seven until ten. At the meeting, defensive strategies were discussed and service rifles offered to farmers if they joined the commando. Because of this commitment, Sally and I barely saw each other until the following evening.

'I'm going with Hannes in the helicopter again,' she said at breakfast. 'It's another psychic thing, and he wants to look around from above.' Not long after she had gone, I paid her cupboard another visit. And there, neatly ruled off in her diary, was the previous day's entry. Sitting down on the bed, I began reading.

It was cool and the electric light shone on the body on the tiled slab. Dressed in white, Dr Fourie was scraping dirt from under the corpse's finger-nails and dropping it into a plastic packet. He stopped when we went in. He and Hannes greeted each other and then I was introduced. I'm the journalist, Hannes said, the one who's doing research for a novel. Dr Fourie seemed nice – quiet and neat. The sight of the dead body made me feel faint but Hannes gave me a stool and stood beside me. The expression on the boy's face was calm despite the mess at his temple where a bullet had entered, and a second bullet hole at his solar plexus, below the horrible '1 Alice, 10 kaffirs' engraving on his chest.

'Look at the hands,' said Dr Fourie, indicating the weals on the palm and between the fingers. 'Defence wounds. He was tortured before they shot him. That inscription,' he continued, pointing at the boy's chest, 'was made before he died.'

'Not nice,' said Hannes.

'No,' said Dr Fourie quietly, probing around the bullet holes and writing on a clipboard.

Once he had finished, Dr Fourie made a Y-shaped incision across the chest with a scalpel. Then, using an electric saw, he cut through the ribs and removed the breastplate. That was when I nearly vomited. The sound of the saw and its hot smell almost turned my stomach. But then something came over me, a sort of second wind. In a shocking way, I suddenly became transfixed by what was happening. As if linked to Dr Fourie's hands, my eyes followed his probing fingers in the boy's meat. When he removed a flattened slug and held it up for us to see, I almost clapped with horror. Hannes put his arm on my shoulder.

After he had again written on the clipboard, Dr Fourie busied himself with the inscription, cutting a piece of the weals with his scalpel, and again writing things down.

'They can spell,' he said. 'That's unusual.'

He then moved from the boy's torso to his head and began to saw open the skull. I could feel myself heave, but kept it down.

'This is the Red Indian part,' he said, smiling briefly.

He levered open the skull and pulled the skin of the scalp from behind the ears, folding it forward across the boy's face. At that point even Hannes looked deathly pale. I could see drops of sweat on his forehead. He burped quietly several times and then sat down on a stool beside me. Dr Fourie removed the crinkled brain and thrust a finger along the route of the bullet until the second slug fell onto the table.

'This is what killed him,' he said, holding up the jagged piece of metal. 'First the writing on the chest, then the two shots. The stomach wound would have killed him eventually but the head wound was very quick.'

I wanted to say something but couldn't open my mouth for fear of gagging.

'Time to put Humpty Dumpty together again,' said Dr Fourie. He then began to return the organs to the chest cavity and placed the brain back in the skull, stitching the incisions coarsely with a black thread.

'Good luck with your book,' he said to me when he was finished. 'I would be interested to read it.'

'I'll send you a copy,' I said, pretending conviction.

Hannes and I then thanked the doctor and left, stopping at the toilets to wash ourselves clean of the morgue. But, no matter how we scrubbed, the sweet smell lingered.

Not feeling up to much else, I accepted when Hannes invited me back to *his flat for coffee. It's the only time I've ever been there. In a funny way, I was stoned by what I had seen – the autopsy I had brought about. That aspect began to dawn on me. How horribly mighty the pen can be!*

Having arrived at his flat, coffee seemed silly, so we began drinking cognac as if the weather was cold and we wanted to warm ourselves. Soon, I was out of it. When Hannes told me to lie down, I went through to his bedroom and found his bed. Feeling dizzy too, he lay down beside me. *

Note the asterisk. After they lay down together. What an indictment! If she were involved in some elaborate deception, how could she be so reckless as to write it down? Perhaps she felt a need to tell it to herself in a peculiar attempt at absolution. Perhaps she thought I would never stray into the depths of her underwear when she wasn't wearing it. Perhaps she thought that if I ever did, I would comment on her diary and thus provide her with the opportunity of brushing aside as presumptuous any conclusions I may have reached.

Whatever the reason, it happened. I caught a glimpse of her state of mind in the morgue and know how she feels. That, I can handle. But the asterisk, that addendum in code set a niggle of doubt going in my head and I carried the puzzle with me to the sheds and irrigation fields until the picture began to emerge. The refusal of sex because of menstruation. The lack of a tampon packet and cardboard cylinder in the bin beside the lavatory where, for as long as I had known her, Sally had discarded them after an insertion after her bath. In my fevered mind, the equation was simple. Mortification at the autopsy had led to a need for reassurance that only the fellow implicated could provide. A drink at Marais' flat. And another. It all pointed to surrender after months of closeness: a brief linkage to seal the bond of guilt. Hence the refusal to do it again that night, using the ploy of a period because she couldn't face the prospect of my entering where Marais had just been. Then the half-confession in her diary because deception had begun to hurt more than complicity in the murder. After all, she had seen the youth gutted – and he wasn't somebody anymore, just a sack of viscera.

It was so clear. Fuck you, Sally, I thought as I returned to the house from the fields. I owe you nothing. This is your family's farm. I can do without it. I can also do without Alice. She's also something of yours. You turned a simple disappearance into a crusade. Go back to Hannes. I'll take myself elsewhere. You're fucked. The country's fucked. I'll make my own way.

My urge to mayhem stirred, but I held myself back. It was time for a dignified departure, not histrionics.

PART TWO

Wanderings

18

And so my wanderings began. I threw some clothes into a backpack, snatched Sally's diary from among her underwear and took my revolver and passport from the safe. Then, without even leaving a note, I left. Glimpsing a duiker in the orchard as I neared the gate, and the black-and-white shimmerings of the cows in the rye grass, I gunned along the farm road towards the highway. Within minutes I was in Bushmansburg. With no future in which to answer for my actions, I parked in a loading zone long enough to convert my savings into travellers' checks. Then, ignoring the ticket on the windscreen, I drove westwards up the hillside and through the mist of the escarpment to the farmlands. The familiar sights of homesteads, silos and herds of Frieslands came into view but all left me cold. Before long, I had climbed Van Reenan's Pass and was in the Orange Free State with its monotonous flatness. Then came the Transvaal. Music and news broadcasts alternated on the radio: Wilson Phillips and *Shakespeare's Sister* punctuated by well-enunciated accounts of murder and mayhem.

With the revolver on the seat beside me, I willed every passerby to be reckless enough to attack. Gone was my studied intention to avoid killing anyone, merely because I had tried not to in Angola during my national service. So great was my agitation that watershed day that I was looking for trouble. The opportunity of blowing somebody away was exciting beyond description. While I couldn't bring myself to shoot in cold blood, I shivered in the hope that someone would be stupid enough to take on a farmer driving alone along that unsafe road. Opening fire and bellowing out my pain, my hatred, my disgust of everything and everyone who had driven me to run for it as I squeezed the trigger again and again until all five chambers were empty, would have been the ultimate catharsis for me.

But the potential attackers remained at bay and I reached Johannesburg without incident. At Jan Smuts Airport, I parked the truck, pushed the revolver under the seat and lugged my pack to International Departures. There, I looked up at the illuminated flight schedule, considering my destination. Not Africa, I told myself. Europe? America? The Far East? I pondered briefly before joining a queue.

As it turned out, my decision was made for me. Without visas, a South African passport is almost useless. But Britain, like a forgiving parent, overlooks the waywardness of its prodigal sons and daughters. So London it was. With only hours before the next flight, and a sudden cancellation, I bought a ticket. I then checked in my luggage and ate a meal in the restaurant, before strolling through the duty-free shops to kill time. The tawdriness of everything revolted me: the kitsch souvenirs, the pulp paperbacks and the newspapers and magazines filled with trivia. But the minutes were ticking away; that was all that mattered.

Take-off was exhilarating. Leaving South African soil for the last time made my heart leap with excitement. With the toy houses and their thumbnail pools receding below, the jumbo maintained its steady ascent and I sat back, waiting for the drinks and losing myself in the piped music. It was dusk and I could see the sun firing the skeins of cloud in long threads of tracer. A good time to leave, I thought, the end of a chapter. Goodbye, Africa! I shouted in my head, seeing myself in my mind's eye on a podium before a multitude. Goodbye for good! I shouted again, and turned and walked away to the sounds of jeers and ululations. Fuck them, I thought. As I knocked back my beers, I earned disapproving glances from two businessmen sitting beside me. Fuck them too, I thought again. As it turned out, they had nothing to fear. I was well-behaved and slept like a child.

Throughout the night we winged high over Africa, sometimes inland, sometimes off the west coast. Before dawn, we sliced Morocco, then arced westwards across the Bay of Biscay. Shortly thereafter, we began our descent, circling slowly above council estates so drab one could weep. But being on the run and buoyed up by my freedom, I was at first immune to the squalor of anything European. My reasoning was simple: I was running away from a great sadness and as long as I kept going there was nothing to fear. We landed with the bump of impact and the rattling rush of engines in reverse, then filed out of the plane into a chill half-light.

Everything was grey whereas only hours before it had been lit by blinding sunlight. But I was buoyed up, on tenterhooks, in overdrive.

I'm out of Africa, I kept telling myself that first day, incredulous that after thirty years I had done it at last. For the first time, I had foreign soil under my feet. English soil. Like my childhood trips to Rhodesia, Swaziland and Lesotho, the Kenyan fortnight hadn't counted. African soil was African soil. But now I had Europe.

With formalities over, I took the tube into London and found a pension near Marble Arch. Offloading my pack, I set off in search of those sights beloved of first-time visitors: Buckingham Palace, Piccadilly Circus, Trafalgar and Leicester Squares, the Tower. Then I visited the museums and galleries, breathless in the National Gallery and Tate because the paintings on display were the real thing – more specifically, because the Bacons and Hockneys in the bookcase back home were reproduced from those originals in front of me.

'Back home.' How that phrase cut me up! In my solitary wanderings around the city, I compared everything to its South African counterpart, most unfavourably at first. For example, pints of bitter tasted weak beside Castle Lager. And the British sun had nothing on our sun, it being winter in the north. Clearly, rejected or not, 'back home' retained its power. And, against my wishes, the pasty women in overcoats couldn't hold a candle to Sally's lithe bronzeness. As I'm sure Marais would agree.

I found a pub not far from the pension and lived off ploughman's lunches. After several pints, I frequently had animated conversations with strangers but none came to anything. One evening a gaunt girl with a tattoo on her neck invited me home but I politely declined, saying I felt sick, which I did. Too much bitter doesn't mix well with bitterness. But I kicked myself afterwards. I could at least have gone along and explored that girl's paleness to spite Sally. But, my luck being what it is, I could also have got myself infected by some Aids-stricken waif to make a futile point. So, remaining rational despite my loneliness, I played safe and went my way.

And then I met Mack, a hearty Australian with a face boiled by sunlight. Of all things, he was a farmer studying ceramics. We became drinking mates, errant sons of the south, discussing anthrax and glazes until late each evening and then staggering back to our rooms. 'Fuck England!' we shouted as the pub doors closed. 'Fuck Australia! Fuck Africa!' And every morning with throbbing heads we went our different ways: Mack back to his clay and me to Kew or Madame Tussauds.

'Tell me about that bird you left behind,' Mack would say well into each evening, his hand unsteady and his eyelids drooping.

'Ah, stuff it,' I would reply each time. 'How many eggs does a kookaburra lay?' And we would keel over with laughter.

My money was going fast. And with my limited savings and the appalling rand/pound exchange rate, I realised I had to do something.

'I'm going to push off into the country,' I told Mack one evening. 'It's too expensive in London.'

'There's no country here like we've got mate,' he replied. 'But go and see for yourself.'

So I did. Promising to look him up when I got back to London, I set off for Cambridge, assuming it to be the essence of England. No sooner had the train left Liverpool Street Station than I was talking to an elderly man in a dark suit, white shirt and striped tie. As it turned out, he was a master at a Hertfordshire public school and his wife had been born in Natal.

'Her parents farmed there,' he said. 'She has very pleasant memories. Bathing under waterfalls and trapping birds with Zulu boys.' God, how it wouldn't leave me alone! I had crossed continents and yet 'back home' was as tenacious as ever. Not just a South African connection, but a Natal one. By the time the train had left suburbia and was clattering through countryside, Andrew Trevelyn and I were acquaintances. He knew me as a South African farmer rather belatedly seeing the world. And I knew him as an English master with a passion for literature and rugby, and a wife from where I came from.

'Do you have an itinerary?' he asked.

'Not really,' I said. 'I've got a three-month visa with ten weeks left. I'm just going where my spirit moves me.'

'Where are you headed now?'

'Cambridge,' I replied.

'Oh, leave Cambridge,' he said, smiling. 'It's just buildings and a river. Come and stay with us. Caroline would so like to meet you. And you could see how a public school works.'

'Thank you,' I said, amazed by his largesse, so at odds with his Englishness and apparent reserve. And surprised also by my prompt acceptance. And so my wanderings took an unexpected turn. As I was to realise later, it was such sudden deviations that made my odyssey so notable. Like a leaf in autumn, I went where the gusts tossed me.

We got off the train at Broxbourne and drove in his Morris towards Hertford. Before we reached the school, its imposing grey facade fronted by columns and topped by a towering dome became visible from across the fields. The Trevelyns lived in a house adjoining the music rooms. Consequently, the happy memories of my four-day stay are punctuated by the muffled trills of pianos and the soft stridency of violins.

In the masculine world of the school, Caroline Trevelyn was a flash of exoticism. Some twenty years younger than her husband, she had dark hair, a razor profile and wore clothes of such rich colours that she seemed a tropical bird darting through the sombre quadrangles. Andrew worshipped her, as did all the boys. With good reason, for she electrified me too. As a part-time French teacher, her timetable was light, and she spent her mornings moving between home and the classrooms. On the two occasions we had tea alone together in the sitting-room, I was mesmerised by her. Of French-Mauritian descent, she was born in Durban and brought up among the sugar fields of the Natal north coast. With our childhoods only a decade and a hundred miles apart, we had much to talk about. She recalled the days of her youth for my endorsement, her eyes often misty from the headiness of certain memories. Cut off when her parents divorced and she moved to France with her mother, her Natal experience was over, like mine, and had the vividness of distance, which mine had still to develop.

From the window in the spare room, I had a view of the rugby fields. Every afternoon, practices were held and I watched Andrew and other masters blow whistles in the murk as the boys scrummed down or ran to and fro passing the ball. On several occasions, Andrew and Caroline took me on tours of the school, from the imposing chapel, hall and dining-room to the library with its Victoria Cross citations and the cloisters with their seemingly endless lists of old boys who had died in battle. Near the classrooms was a Boer War memorial and I thought of all those young

Englishmen who had heeded the call for Queen and Country and were now buried in little cemeteries scattered across the South African veld. With so many memorials, the school had an almost eerie atmosphere, one of a necropolis that prepared youths either for life or a good death in battle.

Where I should go next became a subject of conversation. I told the Trevelyns I wanted to spend another fortnight in England and then head for Europe. After some thought and a telephone call, they had a suggestion: Andrew's brother had a dairy farm on Exmoor. Glad of help, especially from an experienced dairyman, he would give me my board and lodging and a small salary for several weeks. Partly out of gratitude to Andrew and Caroline Trevelyn for their generosity, and partly out of a desire to get back among the muck of byres and the warm smell of milkers, I agreed.

So Cambridge never happened. Instead, I headed back to London, spent a hard night's drinking with Mack, and took the train from Paddington Station. At Taunton, I caught a bus to Minehead, then another to Porlock where I phoned Cyril Trevelyn. Ten minutes later, he arrived in a Land Rover and drove me along winding roads to his farm. Both Cyril and his wife, Diana, were warm but distant. The farmhouse had an easy informality, being cluttered with saddles, gumboots and walking sticks. I was put in a stone cottage beside the garage. Being both private and adjoining the main house, my accommodation was perfect. I enjoyed the best of both worlds.

They worked me hard from dawn to dusk six days a week. It was a sobering experience to be a hired hand. No longer a squire in Africa, I was now seeing things from the other side. Although Cyril Trevelyn was never authoritarian, I was effectively his servant. Like Amos Ntuli, Joseph Mkhize, Moses Sithole and Shorty Ngubane back home, I had to do what I was told.

Working with me were Jimmy Torr and his daughter, Molly. A middle-aged widower, Jimmy had been with the Trevelyn's all his life. He knew everything about the farm, from the genealogy of each cow to the idiosyncracies of every piece of equipment. So to begin with, I worked with him, bringing the milkers in from the fields, chivvying them into the parlour and washing their udders with disinfectant before attaching the clusters of the milking machine. After the morning milking, we drove the cows to the rye

94

grass where an electric fence confined them to a narrow strip as they advanced across each field. Jimmy and I then sluiced the parlour with hoses and busied ourselves with a succession of tasks.

Molly's job was to care for the calves and artificially inseminate the cows on heat. A strapping girl of twenty, she moved through the calf pens in her jeans and anorak, plugging the clamouring mouths with the teats of feeding bottles. Whenever a cow showed signs of oestrus, she and I drove it into the crush-pen. While one of us reassured the animal, the other pushed an arm in its anus and scooped out the dung before locating the cervix through the rectum wall. The plunger and semen straw were then inserted into the vagina. Guided by the hand in the rectum, we found the cervix, positioned the straw and pushed the plunger. An ejaculation of sorts took place and, all being well, the cow conceived.

I took to Molly immediately but she seemed unsure of me at first, clamming up whenever we were together. It seemed more than shyness. Being Britain, class stratifications probably played a part. The Trevelyns were minor gentry and the Torrs working class, with all that that implied. As an outsider, a colonial, I fitted into neither category. On amicable but somewhat distant terms with the Trevelyns, I ate with them and called them by their Christian names. Jimmy and Molly, on the other hand, addressed them as Mr and Mrs Trevelyn and only entered the main house when invited or when work required it.

My first week with the Trevelyns was lonely. Except at meals, I never saw them. They had little to do with the running of the farm, Cyril forever poring over books in his study and Diana posting on a sleek mare in the training ring beside the stables. After a long day with the taciturn Jimmy and cool Molly, I returned alone to my room. Being without transport and exhausted, I lacked the energy to find the nearest pub or read a book. Instead I showered and collapsed on my bed. During my spells of reverie, I saw my parents, both long dead, and thought of my childhood. Inevitably, my nostalgia was overcome by more recent flashes of another sort. A farmhouse battened down for the night. Cattle corralled against rustlers. And a former heroine in the arms of a fascist policeman.

But things soon changed. By the end of the week Molly and I had become friends of sorts. Although we said little to each other, a sense of kinship had developed between us. Whenever Jimmy was away on a tractor, she would materialise beside me in the milking parlour and help guide into the stalls the next relay of milkers. I reciprocated, joining her in the calf-pens with a feeding bottle after each milking session. As calves sucked and nudged the frothy teats, I watched her scratching their curly polls and filling the buckets with starter pellets. Her deftness was remarkable. Barely twenty, she was calm and resourceful, nursing ailing calves, treating infected udders and chastising greedy milkers whenever they lingered in the stalls for more feed concentrate after their milk was finished.

One afternoon early in my second week, I found Molly cleaning the calf-pens. Jimmy was harrowing in the distance and the weak winter sun was sinking behind a crescent of oaks beside the stables. As it was still hours before milking, I offered to help her. 'Thanks,' she said quietly, 'the bedding's dirty. Will you change the water while I open the loft? I'll call you.'

I emptied the muddied buckets into the sluice and watched as they refilled automatically, thin jets of water whining against the plastic sides until the level rose sufficiently for the ball valve to close. Presently, I heard Molly calling. Leaving the nursery, I crossed to the barn and climbed the ladder to the loft. As I reached the top, I saw it all.

Molly was standing naked among the bales. All I can remember in that initial flash was her expanse of dark hair and the white voluptuousness of her breasts and hips.

'Chris,' she said, her arms extended.

I must have paused momentarily because she beckoned with her fingers. Then I stumbled forward, awhirl with confused desire and on the point of tears at the sheer vulnerability of her posture. God, Molly, I remember thinking, what if I had rejected you? But I didn't.

It was all so quick. In seconds I was naked and we were down among the bales. Weeping with gratitude, I covered her with kisses, curling my tongue around her nipples as our groins began their fevered tandem. God! I remember shouting in my mind. God! God! God! as our movements quickened. Then her hair was over me and Molly cried out sharply as I thrust away all the hurt and humiliation of the previous month. With the subsidence came the vacancy of calmness. I rolled off her and lay back with my eyes closed. My mind was hollow and somewhere deep in it a steady refrain was keeping time with my breathing: Sally, Sally, Sally, Sally.

As we lay beside each other, my thoughts cleared slowly and I began to hear the bleating of the calves. Molly sat up and reached for her clothes. As she dressed, I watched her through half-closed eyes, the shapeliness of her legs, buttocks and breasts a paleness above me. Then I too sat up, dragging on my jeans. Before I had finished dressing, Molly was back at work, forking hay from the platform onto the floor below. I stood up and touched her on the arm. As she turned, I kissed her lightly on the lips. 'Thanks Molly,' I said.

'Thanks,' she replied.

And that was that. During my remaining few days, we worked closely together but never once alluded to what had happened. All that had changed was the intimacy of our co-operation. A bond had been formed. On the morning of my departure, with the cows milked and the calves fed, we kissed fleetingly beside the cooling tank and went our separate ways. As I headed back to London and the prospect of pub revels with Mack, I thought of Molly – of her resourcefulness and how much I owed her.

Back among the crowds and traffic, I booked into the same pension that I had inhabited on my arrival from Africa. Then I wandered to Mack's digs and left a note on the door. Being December, the sun had set early and the streetlights shone merrily in the gloom. But the weather was miserable and I felt colder than I had ever felt before. Being alone in London added an iciness of its own. All my residual African warmth had ebbed away and without the rigours of farm labour to generate more, nothing seemed to warm me. Having been paid by the Trevelyns, I eased through the crowds to the nearest travel agent.

'Do you have any cheap flights to Europe?' I enquired of a young woman with glasses. 'To somewhere warm?'

'We've got a special to Barcelona,' she said. 'It's quite warm. It's on the Mediterranean.'

'Fine,' I said, without a second thought.

And so, once again, I found myself blown at random by the winds of fortune. As I left the agency, I was filled with eagerness. Barcelona, I thought, the Olympics, Gaudi. In a city I had never previously considered visiting was where I would be the following evening. The whole notion seemed ridiculously exciting.

I met Mack at a pub at eight. He had a cold and was wrapped in a coat.

'So, what's news?' he asked.

'I set off for Cambridge but never got there. I ended up staying at a public school in Hertfordshire, then worked on a dairy farm in Somerset.'

'Not bad,' he said, nodding.

We ordered drinks. The bar seemed full of theatrical people with scarves and loud voices.

'So how's the countryside?' Mack asked.

'Cold and wet,' I replied.

'That's no lie,' he said. 'I can't take this bloody weather.'

'I'm sick of it too,' I said. 'So I'm going to Barcelona tomorrow.'

'Hey, good move,' he said, his rheuminess dispelled by the alcohol.

The pub served pie and chips, so we ordered and ate and drank. A couple beside us, both actors, introduced themselves and we spent a merry hour talking about ourselves and each other, tracing the many links between Britain, South Africa and the Antipodes.

'Have you heard from your bird back home?' Mack asked after the couple had left.

'What about the kookaburra eggs?' I replied, reviving my old counter and making light of something that wasn't.

At closing time we left quietly, lacking the energy for pavement execrations.

'Keep in contact,' said Mack as we went our separate ways. 'Maybe I'll join you.'

'Cheers,' I said. 'I'll phone you from Spain.'

19

I landed in Barcelona late in the afternoon. Although warmer than London, it was also drizzling and grey. Thanks to the Olympics, the airport and the train to the city centre were new and clean. Using a guidebook, I found a pension near Catalunya Square. My room was small and dingy. Being tired, I lay down on my bed with my sleeping bag over me. Then, for the umpteenth time since I had left home, I wondered how my departure had been received. Was there drama? Were the police called? Was Sally anguished? Or did she only pretend anguish, knowing that she was now free to take up openly with Marais? What had been Will's reaction? Had he moved into the main house? In fact, had anyone missed me? After pondering these thoughts for a time, I ate a box of shortbread and drank a beer. Then I fell asleep.

Next morning, I wandered around the city centre, orientating myself. Everything, I discovered, was exorbitantly expensive. Also, the Spaniards seemed self-absorbed and their language was unintelligible. Feeling very alone, I allocated myself only two days to see the sights before moving on.

Visible over the rooftops was the Sagrada Familia, Gaudi's towering Temple of the Holy Family. I set off along the streets towards the spires and spent several hours there. What surprised me at first was the building's incompleteness; cranes and scaffolding grew like weeds between the branching spires. It was amazing to me that this structure, worked on intermittently for over a century, was still so far from completion. Overpowered by Gaudi's vision, I lost myself briefly in the mad ornateness of the decorations. Like swallows on a telegraph wire, a string of Japanese tourists chattered along a lofty bridge, their cameras busy. Couples kissed and laughed beneath the vine-tendrils and leaf-clusters of a portal depicting the Nativity. Deep in my anorak, I made my way between them, longing to share my reactions with Sally but having to manage alone.

At dusk the Ramblas came alive. Waves of people meandered

down the wide mall, funneling between the kiosks selling birds and newspapers as lights flickered from the bare branches of the winter trees. It was drizzling when I joined the throng, pausing to hear a group of Peruvian troubadors, then watch a mime artist dressed in black enact a sequence of the Grim Reaper scything lives. Family groups walked arm-in-arm, the senoras wrapped in furs. Many of the young women were beautiful. But similarly dressed, I told myself, Sally would have eclipsed them all. I wondered what she was doing at that moment. Give or take an hour, she would have left the paper. Had she returned to the farm? Or was she with Marais propping up some bar, or worse?

I had a sandwich and a beer, then carried on down the Ramblas towards the harbour. Two Australian girls asked me to take a photograph of them, which I did, but they left before I could begin a conversation. I drank another two beers in a bar. Each cost a bomb and I finished them quickly, having no place to sit and no-one to talk to. Outside, American sailors advanced in groups, their voices strident. As I moved on, so my sense of solitariness increased. Why am I never like this in Africa? I remember asking myself. Why can I be alone there but never feel alone?

A song's refrain kept coming to mind. It was an early *Doors* number about people being strange when one's a stranger, and seeming ugly when one's alone. I played with the words as I walked, reciting them in my head: 'Women seem wicked when you're unwanted, streets are uneven when you're down.' So closely did the sentiments express my own that I took heart, finding a perverse pleasure in my kinship with the lyricist who wrote them. Both of us, I remember feeling, know what it's like.

Near the harbour, I turned and headed back up the mall. Not far beyond the Liceu opera house, a liveried doorman outside a plush hotel beckoned me. We exchanged pleasantries, and then he asked: 'Have you got money?'

'Yes, some,' I said.

'You need company. I know a very nice woman. Wait here.'

He entered the hotel and I could see him making a call from a booth near the reception desk. Presently he returned and handed me a map drawn on a piece of paper.

'It's not far,' he said. 'She is waiting for you. Have a good time. You will thank me.'

Unsure how to respond, I thanked him.

'It is a favour,' he said, pointing up the street towards Catalunya Square. 'You must go up there.'

'Okay,' I nodded, recklessly compliant, and set off through the light rain.

I found her easily. She was, I suppose, typically Catalan with her fair skin and dark hair. Silver rings hung from the lobes of her ears. Using broken English and our fingers, we negotiated a price. I could ill afford it, but paid.

The room was warm and scented. She drew the curtains and took off her clothes. She was buxom and decorated with tattoos: hearts over her nipples and a cornucopia spiralling into her navel. I undressed slowly, removing each garment in a deliberate way.

'You English?' she asked falteringly.

'South African,' I said.

She raised her eyebrows. '*Sudafrica?*'

'Yes.'

She touched my skin. 'So white.'

'Yes,' I smiled.

She removed a condom from its wrapping and unravelled it. 'Come,' she said. I stood beside her, smelling the spicy fragrance of her hair. Then she lay on a bed and drew up her legs, parting them.

'Come,' she said again, stretching out a hand and drawing me by the arm. I knelt on the bed. Fondling me with one hand, she drew me onto her. I lowered myself and her legs encircled me.

I felt a sudden impulse to kiss her but somehow it seemed immoral. The roles were reversed, the orifices switched, her mouth withheld while her legs remained splayed. As I had to remind myself, I was merely a customer moving up to my release before withdrawing, leaving her to close and freshen herself in anticipation of her next encounter.

'You nice,' she said professionally and I felt an urge to return the compliment but exchanging niceties seemed equally inappropriate. Her warmth and softness, I told myself, are part of the package. After an indifferent climax, I stood up, removed the condom and dropped it into a plastic bucket in the corner. She slipped on a gown as I dressed.

'*Adios Sudafrica*,' she said as I opened the door.

Cold thrust in as I stepped outside. Catalunya Square and the

101

Ramblas glistened with wetness and I watched my dark shape slip across the speckled neons shimmering on the pavement. I remember peering for features but being confronted only by the dark emptiness of my silhouette.

Yet again, I sought a bar. Like all the others, it was warm and crowded. There was music, and men and women were laughing. Standing near the door, I knocked back a whisky and then stepped outside. It was cold and still raining. I headed back to the pension, unfulfilled and hating myself for squandering my money.

In my room, I pulled on a tracksuit and slipped down the passage to the shower, relishing the hot water and the smell of the soap. Then I fell on my bed and was asleep within minutes.

During the night the weather changed. At dawn it was still drizzling and an iciness had set in. Encased in my anorak, I drank a cup of coffee and ate a pastry before searching for the cathedral. Whether it was my guidebook's recommendations or a sense of contrition that drove me there, I don't know, but I headed back down the Ramblas and bore leftwards to a smallish square outside the cathedral entrance. Passing beggars on the steps, I went inside.

It was dark and cavernous. People moved about in the hushed gloom: to and from the pews, or along the aisles to the barred sanctuaries with their relics and gilded statuary. In the darkness near the door a woman was selling candles and I approached the bank of flickering orange, enjoying its warmth and waxy fragrance and extending my hands towards the guttering wicks so their shadow patterns played across my skin. It was magical, fairy-like. As I stood transfixed, with devotees shuffling around me in the shadows, the warm, shimmering orangeness became a glow of subtropical memories. As though on celluloid, I saw a jumble of images from home: waves on hot beaches, chameleons on bougainvillaea, butterflies above pools and Sally laughing, laughing, with the sun behind her. Glimpses of paradise.

Eventually, I crossed to the pews and sat down. High above me loomed the vault on its huge, fluted columns. Absorbed by the shuffling ebb and flow of elderly women, crossing themselves and muttering incantations, I sat in a state of calm reverie. Below the altar was a crypt into which a stream of pilgrims was descending, feeding money into a meter for lighting. While the light snapped on and off, a priest appeared at the pulpit and for the next hour intoned in

102

Spanish. It was afternoon when I left. Outside it was raining steadily. Pulling forward the hood of my anorak, I headed back to the pension.

As I had seen so clearly in the glow of candlelight in the cathedral, it was Africa, not Europe, that I was seeking. Not darkest Africa as such, but my Africa. I was no longer sure what that was. Sally was part of it, as was Alice, but it went beyond individuals. I knew that my search was for a fragile limbo where the Old and New Worlds meet. Not raw Africa, but a tamer one with the possibility of rawness. A feeling of ambiguity characterised it: a consciousness of being here but not here, a foundness and lostness. So even if Barcelona had donned all her finery, I had to reject her. I needed to.

So when I found myself back among the grey trees of the Ramblas, I felt more lonely than ever. 'Go home,' a voice said, 'don't waste your life-savings on nothing.' At a low ebb, I resolved to phone Mack, as promised. We could have some good laughs together. Armed with a pocketful of coins, I set off in search of a telephone. No sooner had I reached Catalunya Square than a small man appeared beside me. 'Hello,' he said. 'You Australian?'

'No,' I replied. 'South African.'

'Oh,' he said, surprised. 'I used to do business in your country. In Cape Town.'

Perhaps I looked incredulous, because he continued: 'I sell leather products – shoes, jackets. But the demand for our products has declined in South Africa. Your currency is too weak now.'

'I know,' I said, 'everything's so expensive here.'

'For you,' he said, smiling. 'Spain has come a long way in a few years.' Then, with a start, as if remembering suddenly, he stopped walking. 'This is my daughter,' he announced. A plump girl with glasses and a star of David on a chain around her neck emerged from behind her father and smiled shyly.

'Hello,' I said.

'Ah yes,' said the man. 'I hear you have more trouble in South Africa.'

'When?' I asked.

'It was on the television yesterday.'

'I don't know what's happening,' I said. 'I've been away for a month.'

'Oh, so you haven't heard. A car was ambushed. Some European people were killed.'

'Tourists?' I asked.

'No,' he said. 'South Africans like you.'

'Where?'

'In Natal Province, I think.'

'I'm from Natal,' I said.

'Then you must phone your family and find out.'

'I was looking for a phone when I met you.'

'No, no,' he exclaimed. 'You must phone from my business. It will be cheaper than a call box and you can pay me afterwards.' He swept me along, his plump daughter scurrying beside us. 'When I was young, terrible things happened to my people. So you must keep in touch with your family.' He looked at me. When I nodded, he continued in a lighter vein. 'I have many happy memories of South Africa. I have friends there, you see. Durban, it is in Natal?' He glanced at me.

'Yes,' I said.

'The Davidsons. They used to live in Cape Town. I haven't seen them for many years. You know them?'

'No,' I said.

Wait, I checked myself. What's happening? Why the persistent interest? It can't just be friendliness. And yet, in a funny way, I wanted to play along, not through naivety but because my encounter with the strange little man and his reticent daughter was the most personal I'd had since I left England.

We weaved through the afternoon shoppers before entering a high-rise building and taking the lift up several floors. When the doors opened we were in a large pink room cluttered with racks of leatherware and mirrors. There appeared to be no customers but a bevy of employees bustled about, opening and closing packages, rearranging displays, dusting. All showed my companion the greatest respect, the women curtseying and the few men bowing whenever he addressed them. Turning to a young woman behind a counter, he said something in Spanish and she dialled a number on the telephone and spoke briefly.

'She is getting the code for South Africa,' he said. 'What is your number?'

Instinctively, I gave him the farm's number and its area code. He babbled an order. The woman dialled and then beckoned and handed me the phone. The receiver smelt of perfume. Within the hollow resonance, I heard the telephone ringing. Then it stopped and I heard Sally's voice.

'Hello,' she said. When I remained silent, she said it again: 'Hello.' In the background I heard a muffled voice, to which Sally responded, quietly and away from the mouthpiece: 'There's no answer. It's probably him again.' Then, almost imperceptibly, I heard the call of a nightjar in the background, the familiar quavering litany. I replaced the receiver.

'No reply?'

'Just the answering machine,' I said.

'Too bad,' said the man. 'But the machine is a good sign. If there had been any trouble it would have been broken or someone else would have answered.'

'I suppose so,' I said. 'What do I owe you?'

'No conversation, no charge.'

'Are you sure?'

He nodded. 'It's a pleasure my friend. Cape Town has already paid me with happy memories: the harbour, the mountain, the people.'

I thanked him, said goodbye and took the lift down to the street. It had started raining, and Sally's voice echoed in my head as I began to walk along the pavement. So she was still at home. But who was with her? Will? Marais? And who was she referring to? Marais, possibly. Or some other sinister caller whom she may think is me. But why didn't she just say: 'Chris, is that you?' That was all I needed. Just the assurance that Marais was a passing fancy brought on by circumstances. And that she was terribly sorry. Tears would have helped, and terms of endearment.

And the nightjar. So often, as Sally and I sat together in the sitting-room in the evenings, we had heard the same liquid notes through the window. On occasions when I walked Will back to his cottage, I had almost stepped on the mottled bird before it flapped awkwardly away into the darkness. Over the years it had become a source of reassurance, there on quiet nights but not when the moon was full and the dogs were restless. In a way, that I had heard it was both good and bad. Good that all was well, but bad that all continued to be well without my presence.

I made my way back to the pension and fell on the bed. Cars swished past on the wet street outside. I rose and closed the shutters and drew the curtains to exclude the noise. It was dark and quiet and cold. In my jumbled thoughts, Sally, the nightjar and Africa became a single wistful spectre and I wept myself to sleep at the lostness of it all.

20

At some point during my half-sleep that night, I made the decision: I must return to Africa immediately. Checking out of the pension early, I spent the morning arranging a Moroccan visa and then booked my ticket to Algeciras from where the ferry leaves for Tangier.

The evening train was bursting. Eight of us were crammed into a second-class compartment. While we helped each other pack our luggage on racks and under seats, nodding thanks and smiling, I noted my fellow travellers: two Moroccan youths, two Spanish soldiers, two elderly Hispano-American sisters and a young blonde woman of unknown nationality. No sooner had the train started than the Moroccan youths fell asleep and the conscripts left for the bar in the dining car. While the elderly sisters busied themselves with sandwiches, talking animatedly to each other in English and Spanish, the blonde took a book by Katherine Mansfield from her backpack and began reading it. As Sally had Mansfield books at home, and as I knew from them that she was a New Zealander, I took a long shot.

'You must be a Kiwi,' I said.

'Yes,' she smiled.

'I'm from South Africa.'

'Hi,' she said.

'Are you on holiday?' I asked.

'I've been studying in England,' she replied. 'I'm visiting Morocco on my way home.'

She ventured nothing more and resumed her reading. She was very pretty: slight and blonde and blue-eyed. Another Alice. The resemblance was uncanny. She was older, of course, but strikingly similar in appearance to the young woman Alice Walker would have been in a few years' time if she hadn't gone for a walk and vanished into thin air.

The train clattered through the night. By consensus, at ten

o'clock we switched off the lights and tried to sleep. Some time later, the national servicemen returned noisily from the bar and collapsed in their seats, one of them snoring in a manner reminiscent of James Leonard. After a fitful sleep, I awoke at dawn to see scattered buildings flashing past. Then the train slowed and stopped at Algeciras Station, amidst the tracks and grass and the sad jumble of railway clutter.

I snatched a coffee at the station cafe and then tailed the Moroccans towards the harbour. A large white ferry was moored beside the quay. After an interlude of queueing and regulations, I found myself aboard as the ferry cast off and Algeciras and the nearby brooding bulk of Gibraltar began to recede beyond the dissolving wake.

Once we were out at sea, all passengers had to present their passports to a Moroccan official. When my turn came, the officer pored over my particulars, scrutinising my photograph and visa.

'*Afrique du Sud?*' he queried belligerently.

'Yes,' I replied.

There was a pause. Then, pocketing my passport, he waved me away.

'I have a visa,' I said.

'*Tanger,*' he snapped.

'South Africans can visit Morocco now,' I added lamely.

'*Tanger! Tanger!*' he shouted, dismissing me with a flap of his hands. I climbed dejectedly to the top deck. Returning to Africa, it seemed, wasn't going to be easy. Although Morocco had officially opened its doors to South Africans, our pariah status was dying hard. 'Fuck you all,' I thought as the Spanish coastline gave way to the shores of Barbary.

Symbolically, I suppose, I belong somewhere in the Straits of Gibraltar: adrift on that fluid highway between two continents, nearer Africa but belonging fully to neither. As a white South African I was as lost as Alice. But now I was returning to my home continent in the hope that I could feel at home there.

Before long, Tangier appeared: a slope of white buildings above a sweeping bay. As the ferry headed for the terminal, the vista composed. To the west was the breakwater, thrusting into the straits like a bush-knife. Above it were the *medina* and kasbah. Eastwards, on the hillside, was the *ville nouvelle* and, below and beyond, the serration of beach hotels.

No sooner had we moored than a gangplank was attached and the passengers began to disembark. Without a passport, I found myself on deck with several other misfits, each awaiting our fate. Among us was a Haitian without a visa. Two looked Scandinavian; another, Middle Eastern. A foolhardy Israeli, perhaps. When several officials appeared, the Haitian was told he was being sent back to Spain. Before hearing about the others, I was escorted into the depths of the terminal building. There, several officials scrutinised me through narrow eyes, asked a few questions in broken English, and then waved me though.

Even before I emerged into the glare of the esplanade, the hustlers descended. A pack surrounded me, each insisting that I accept his services. Warned by my guidebook, I declined them all. Instead, having memorised a map of the city centre, I headed off up the hillside, between the walls of the old Jewish cemetery and the *medina*. Battered Citroens and Renaults edged through the throng. Arab men passed, staring. Arab women glanced away demurely. Impassive Berbers squatted beside their stalls. And still a single hustler shadowed me, babbling aggressively in Arabic and broken English.

'Leave me alone, please. I know where I'm going. I don't need your help,' I said repeatedly, wanting to tell him to fuck off but being prudent.

Some distance up the hill I noticed an altercation beside a flight of steps where hawkers were displaying their wares. Several hustlers, it appeared, had surrounded a woman, yapping like wild dogs around a stricken gazelle. As I neared, I saw it was the New Zealander.

I moved quickly. 'Let's go,' I said, taking her by the arm. 'She's with me,' I added icily. 'We don't need your help.' As I said it, that old impulse for mayhem stirred as it had when I read of Sally's unfaithfulness and wanted to express myself violently. All I needed was a firearm and I would have done something very rash. The hustlers must have sensed I meant business because they withdrew.

Taking her backpack, I led her by the arm up the steps, past rows of passive witnesses. Three blocks later, I found my destination: the Hotel Paris. We were given a room overlooking the street. It had a bathroom en suite and a balcony, and its floor was covered in an intricate mosaic.

'My name is Anna,' said the girl. Then she lay down on the bed and fell asleep. Feeling weary myself, I too lay down. From across the bed she looked very beautiful.

I remember lying watching her and thinking rather melodramatically: do you know who I am? I'm one of the world's pariahs. A perpetrator of a crime against humanity. I've been a soldier too. While I may not have killed anyone, I've done my fair share of maiming. So I'm also sick, you could say. Or a victim of circumstances, born into a threatened minority at the southern tip of Africa. And here you are, so trusting. We've only known each other for minutes, yet you are asleep beside me in a strange room in a strange country. But you needn't fear. I'll look after you. I'll guard you with my life.

With hindsight, this seems an attempt at penitence. I'm paraphrasing, of course, but I remember the mood. Nowadays I am easier with myself, more accepting of who I am.

Waking before Anna, I crossed to the balcony and settled myself in an old deck chair to watch the activity in the street. Cars inched, bumper-to-bumper. Pedestrians crammed the pavements – the men either in *djellabas* or western clothes, but all the women traditionally dressed, some veiled, some with their faces exposed. Groups of men lounged at tables at the sidewalk cafes, drinking mint tea and watching the passing parade. As the shadows lengthened, several Berber women, their butter-pink faces shining in the light, appeared among the clothes-lines on a nearby rooftop, laughing and talking as they peered and pointed at the movement below. Shortly before Anna awoke, when the cars had turned on their lights and the street had assumed a festive air, what appeared to be a Jewish congregation emerged from a large building opposite the hotel. Soberly dressed, they dispersed in the twilight – perhaps the remnants of the Jewish mercantile community that had fled Tangier when the port had lost its international status decades earlier.

As I watched the discordant display, I found myself embracing it instinctively. Notwithstanding my brush with the passport official, the hustlers, and the Anna incident, it was a tonic to be back in Africa. The harsh sunlight, the dust, the poverty, the vigour of a racial polyglot and the brooding threat of terrible violence were all part of me. Speaking neither French nor Arabic didn't matter. What counted was that I could sense Africa. Like my knowledge of the smell and feel of Sally's body, it was a delicate empathy borne of time and great intimacy. Whether one is in Morocco or Kenya or South Africa, the continent feels the same. But Tangier has an added advantage. The rankness of the deep interior is tempered by the sight of Europe across the narrow strait: not home, but like a hospital ship anchored offshore.

Anna was disorientated when she awoke. With her hair tousled, she went through to the bathroom. When she reappeared, she joined me on the balcony.

'How're you feeling?' I asked.

'Fine,' she said. 'Thanks.'

As the sun sank into the Atlantic, the Berber women on the opposite roof vanished among the gently palpitating walls of laundry. Down in the street, the crowds had increased, seething through the shimmering lights.

'Why are you in Morocco?' I asked.

'I was at Cambridge on a scholarship,' she said, 'studying bores like Chaucer and Langland. It was cold and raining. Then one night I saw the movie *The Sheltering Sky* and thought "I want to go there." So I left.'

'And here you are.'

'Yes, but it wasn't just the movie. I had read Paul and Jane Bowles. And Canetti and Burroughs. And Anthony Burgess's *Earthly Powers*. My older sisters had Crosby, Stills and Nash records and played *Marrakesh Express* endlessly when I was a kid. And we had big, glossy Moroccan oranges at Cambridge. I had this romantic picture in my head. I wanted to see it.'

'Have you found it yet?'

'Maybe a bit.' Anna smiled ironically. She took a joint from her pocket and lit it.

'A month ago I was heading for Cambridge,' I said. 'But I got side-tracked. I hear it's very beautiful.'

'Very pretty,' she said. 'Where you from in South Africa?'

'Natal.' And I told her about Sally and the farm and how we had had an argument and I had decided it was time to see the world.

'When are you going back?' she asked.

'I don't know.'

She drew on the joint.

'What are your plans?' I asked.

Anna shrugged. 'Just get around, I suppose. And yourself?'

'The same,' I said.

I took a shower while Anna read on the balcony, holding her Katherine Mansfield book at an angle to catch the lamplight through the French doors. She then showered and we went out in search of a place to eat. Not far from the hotel we found a small restaurant where we ate chicken and olives. Later, we came across the Tangerinn, a bar in the Hotel El Muniria where we discovered the Beat writers had stayed and William Burroughs had written *The Naked Lunch*. Although I had never heard of Burroughs, Anna was excited by the literary connection. We ordered beers from an Arab youth behind the counter. All the other drinkers, I noticed, were expatriates and Anna was the only woman. The lighting was dim and rosy and on the wall was a large portrait of a young cavalry-man with his plumed helmet.

'Who's that?' Anna asked the barman, pointing at the photo-graph.

He gestured towards an elderly man in a chair in the corner.

'He's part-owner,' said a small man with a French accent who was sitting beside us. 'He used to be in the British Army. The Household Cavalry.'

Dressed in slippers and a paisley dressing-gown, the old cavalry-man appeared frail and detached. From time to time the barman brought him a drink and patrons crossed to his chair and paid court briefly before returning to the bar.

'You just arrived?' asked a man wearing glasses who appeared behind the counter.

'Yes,' said Anna.

'Your first visit?'

'Yes.'

'You travelling together?' He looked at me.

'Yes,' I said.

'I was going to travel alone,' said Anna.

The elderly man nodded.

'Is it all right for a woman to travel alone in Morocco?' Anna asked.

'It's been done before,' said the man. The barman whispered something in his ear and he glanced at two men in the far corner of the room before continuing. 'But there's a golden rule here. Trust nobody. Especially anyone who becomes friendly too quickly.'

'You been here long?' I asked.

'Years,' he said.

'And Tangier?'

He shrugged. 'It depends what you like.'

'What should we see?' asked Anna.

The man paused. 'The *medina*. The kasbah. St Andrew's church. If you're interested in Matisse, the Hotel Villa de France, although it's closed now. If there's something special you want, you have to ask for it.'

'Like what?' asked Anna.

'You tell me,' he said.

We left before midnight. Being mid-December, the night was cool. We picked our way through dark and littered alleys to the hotel. Back in the room, Anna produced another joint and we smoked it on the balcony. It was ironic that after years of dismissing Zulu labourers for smoking dagga, I was smoking it myself. But I was still rational enough to pretend that things were different.

When we'd finished the joint, we sat silently together in the Tangerine night. The street was empty. I took deep breaths, both to clear my head and intoxicate myself with the stink of Africa. Then we climbed into bed. I was soon asleep. Sometime during the night Anna said she was cold.

'Come in with me,' I said, as if in a dream.

21

Anna and I spent four days in Tangier. Being either stoned or hung-over, our sightseeing was slow and desultory. First, we drifted to the *medina*, weaving through the labyrinth with its teetering buildings, peering into sweatshops and communal bakeries, and seeking those areas that bolstered Anna's romantic notion of the city: the Petit Socco with its once-legendary bars, and the surrounding alleys where the straight and gay brothels had thrived in the international days. During our ramblings, we noticed members of the Tangerinn brotherhood either cruising or sitting alone at the sidewalk cafes, each eyeing the passing trade. Then we climbed to the kasbah and gazed from the ancient crenellated walls of the fort at the sea and the bush-knife breakwater with its scabbard of waves.

The glare was fierce and through squinting eyes the *medina's* maze became Lamu or downtown Mombasa. Here again was that peculiar blend of beauty and squalor; that paradise enriched by the hell within it. As we weaved through the warren, I was a comber on Lamu's beach, hushed by the whispering palms and stirred by the muezzin's nasal cry from across the Shela rooftops. And in the nights of my reverie I was entwined with Sally beneath a mosquito net, awash with fever until our clamouring release.

Each evening we found a restaurant in the *ville nouvelle*, either near our hotel or down the hillside towards the beach. After meals of couscous with brochettes, or chicken and olives, we returned to the Tangerinn, tippling with the restless cruisers until late in the night. Under the vague gaze of the pyjamaed ex-cavalryman, we learnt of the city-within-the-city, having our Tangier observations honed by the old hands. Then, it was back to the hotel balcony for a joint or merely to breathe the foetid fragrance of the African night.

And so I led Anna through the city. Being a free spirit, she was forever willing, happily meandering in search of romance while I delved for some proof that I was more than an expatriate in Africa. But Anna wasn't just drifting vacantly; she was working at a journal, pulling it from her bag intermittently and scribbling. And I soon followed suit. Like Sally in Kenya, I began to record everything, but not because I was determined to preserve aspects of a foreign country. Instead, I broke up my account into confessions of sorts to Sally and Alice, all of them littered with snippets from that other life I had so recently left behind.

Anna was too preoccupied with her mythical Morocco to be bothered with my efforts. This was just as well because I was taking liberties. In some of my monologues, I excluded her entirely while in others she was a lover with whom I entwined in an assortment of exotic settings. Why I did this, I don't know. Perhaps in some irrational way I was hoping to rile Sally; but this was nonsensical because she was a continent away. In short, they were nothing more than self-indulgent flights of fancy that in some obtuse way helped me keep my lostness at bay. Let me explain.

Each began by placing me in time and space. This meant a sequence of dates and locations: my getaway flight from Johannesburg, followed by London, Hertfordshire, Somerset, Barcelona, and Morocco. And, depending on my intended recipient, my persona ranged from braggart to supplicant. For example, Sally heard all about Molly in the hayloft and the Catalan senorita with a tattoo in her navel – but only simplistically. She even got flashes of Anna in imagined couplings in mosques and smoky dens. Alice, on the other hand, had to settle for philosophical puzzles and interminable questions.

I even linked locales to the farm so Sally had to understand. For example, being unsure that she would know were Tangier is, I used a homegrown simile. Remember (I said) you mentioned that the dam below the rye grass fields looks like a map of Africa? Well, if you're near the pumphouse, I'm now up near the blackwood tree where Will shot the cobra. Then she had to know exactly where I was.

And I also took her sightseeing, following in Anna's and my footsteps – to the Hotel Villa de France and St Andrew's Anglican Church. The hotel (I told her) is closed now but it's where Matisse stayed when he visited Tangier. Through locked wrought-iron gates you can glimpse wide steps crowded by palms and undergrowth. The hotel has a broad white facade with lines of windows with green shutters. Matisse always stayed in Room 35 and I imagined you looking at the shutters and trying to decide which one it was. It had to be in front because he painted views through his window of the church and the *medina* and the sea. You could either look among the art books in the hall or go to the Bushmansburg Library and trace Matisse in the card catalogue and see what I am seeing. It would be strange – your looking at it there and thinking that what Matisse had drawn is what I am seeing here so many years later.

St Andrew's Anglican Church is just down the hill from the Villa de France. You won't believe it but there's litter and shit right outside its gates. The church is a subtle blend of Arabian and European while the churchyard is hidden from the busy street and is cool and wooded. There are graves of prominent members of Tangier's expatriate community: journalists, soldiers and even an Englishwoman who married a shereef. You would find it marvellously romantic – death, quietness, greenery, foreign names on mossy stones.

But for me, the graves were just forgotten people far from home. Or at home? Who knows?

In Sally's case, each chunk of tailor-made travelogue was followed by a glimpse of Anna, always beautiful and compliant. And the tableaux I conjured were designed to titillate: Anna without underwear beside minarets; Anna bare-breasted smoking a joint on an ornate balcony; Anna sitting heavily on my lap in a dim bar. In fact Anna was the link-pin between my two approaches, alternately Sally's arch-rival and an Alice clone.

My Alice letters couldn't have been more different. In her case, my tone was imploring, hesitant and strewn with questions like the perennial what happened on that fateful summer's day when you put on a swimming costume under your clothes, draped a yellow towel across your shoulders, and walked out of the gate arched with roses?

And, as so often before, I asked the other questions we have all asked: Marais, Sally, myself and everyone else who has been haunted by the fate of Alice Walker. Were you only going swimming or were the costume and towel simply a ruse to deflect from another intention? Were you headed for an assignation in a house nearby or in the gully of bush that you may have chosen to cross rather than take the connecting road higher up the hillside? Was there a vehicle waiting, one that you were expecting?

Or was it merely an innocent outing to a neighbour's pool that went horribly wrong? Perhaps there was a stranger, beckoning quietly from an idling car. And like the well-brought-up girl you are, you approached the open window with the smiling face behind the dark glasses. Or was it a loiterer in the undergrowth, a Pan with his pipe whose advances you were powerless to spurn?

Perhaps there was even a snake in that wild garden: a sudden strike from the foliage and a terrifed girl flailing about among the rocks and maidenhair fern until the toxin brought on paralysis. Perhaps stray dogs and the deluge that night effected the dispersal before the police could bring themselves to act.

Or should we see your fate symbolically? As a glimpse of all our lostnesses, now and to come?

Oh, Alice, speak to me!

At times I even explained to her why I was going on so. The explanation is simple. It is a matter of causation. Alice's vanishment, through a tenuous sequence of events, led to my flight and sojourn in Morocco. In other words, Alice, I am who I am because of you.

Back in our room after seeing the St Andrews Church cemetery, I began thinking about those expatriates whose graves Sally and I had found in Kenya and asked myself if they belonged in Africa. What of Baden-Powell who turned down Westminster Abbey for Nyeri cemetery? To choose the lee of Mount Kenya rather than England's holiest of holies for his resting place must surely qualify him for naturalisation. And Jim Corbett? Being born in India and dying in Kenya, he was a man of heat and dust. Breathing your surroundings should be qualification enough. Understanding is belonging.

And Sally? With blood on her hands, she was different from me. But whatever her culpability, what she did next was crucial. If she stayed in Natal, she could join the ranks of those who belong. If she ran away, she would find herself like me in a double bind: an expatriate expatriate. And Marais? Fuck him. And Alice? God knows.

Across the street the Berber women were back on the rooftop among their laundry. Africa's only white indigenous tribe, if you exclude the likes of me, they had been reduced to servility by the Romans and Arabs. But they seemed happy enough, those women with their butter-pink faces and their ready laughter.

22

On our last day in Tangier, we left the hotel before dawn and lugged our backpacks down to the station on the esplanade. The sea looked grey in the half-light. People stirred in doorways, some sweeping, some just standing and smoking. Reaching the station, we cut through the throng in the concourse and boarded the train. Although the second-class compartment was crowded, Anna and I found seats by a window. We kept to ourselves, Anna reading while I stared abstractedly at the late arrivals running anxiously along the platform.

Soon we were off, skirting the wide arc of the bay and then slicing southwards into the interior. I looked out of the window as Tangier's muddle gave way to grassland and gum trees. The slow movements of livestock and country people seemed typically African. Whether kikuyu tillers or Zulu or Arab herdsmen, Africa's players follow the same slow drum beat.

As we descended the Atlantic seaboard and turned eastwards into the Middle Atlas, I was struck by the quality of Moroccan agriculture: meticulous groves of oranges and olives, plots of lush vegetables and sleek herds of sheep and cattle. Some of the scenery in the hinterland was almost Drakensberg-like with its slopes and greenness and rushing streams.

We reached Fez in the afternoon. No sooner had we left the station and begun our tentative advance into the city than a youth appeared and tagged along. Despite our entreaties to be left alone, he shadowed us to the centre of the *ville nouvelle* where we soon discovered that all the hotel rooms were taken. The youth was full of suggestions but we heeded the advice of the Tangerinn proprietor and pressed on, eventually finding a seedy establishment that had a vacancy.

Our room was drab and dirty. With the window hidden by a heavy blind which refused to open, we had to use the electric light although the sun was still shining outside. The naked bulb gave the threadbare pink bedspread the livid glow of a ripening boil. The bed stank of cheap perfume and Anna pulled down the top sheet to reveal a spattering of pubic hairs.

'This place's a brothel,' she said. 'I'm not putting my little toe in there.'

We then unrolled our sleeping bags on the bed. I lay down on my bag, taking trouble to avoid touching the bedspread, while Anna crossed to the en-suite bathroom.

'The toilet's leaking,' she announced. 'The floor's all wet.'

'Let's go and get something to eat,' I said.

The wide streets were quiet. Near the hotel a few people were sitting at tables beside a small shop with a display of fruit and a stand of faded postcards. Finding no restaurant, we settled for a *patisserie* and indulged in coffee and croissants.

Later, we returned to the hotel and bathed, using two mats from the bedroom as stepping stones on the bathroom floor. Afterwards Anna took a joint from her bag and we lay down on the bed and smoked it as the shadows lengthened through the slatted blinds.

'That Alice you told me about,' said Anna. 'Where do you really think she is?'

'I don't know,' I said.

'You must have some idea,' she persisted.

'It depends on how I feel,' I said. 'If I'm up, she's alive. If I'm down, she's dead.'

'She's like rain,' said Anna. 'She's what you want her to be.'

I drew deeply on the joint and passed it back to Anna. In the haze of pungent smoke I thought of the sound of rain drumming on the corrugated-iron roof of my bedroom when I was a child. Down the passage I could hear the muffled voices of my parents. It was dark but my Meccano windmill was just visible on a table beside my cupboard. I drew on the joint again and passed it to Anna. She drew heavily on it. Then I drew on it again and passed it back. Everything was slow and clear. Anna was beautiful. I looked at her blonde hair and the way it fell in strands. I focused on the gold earring in the soft lobe below the delicate whorls of her ear. Lobes: I said the word to myself. Lobes. The room was quiet. My mind was quiet. I laughed softly.

'What's the joke?' asked Anna.

'Lobes,' I said.

'Lobes?'

'Yes,' I said.

Anna laughed. Then she just lay on her back beside me and stared at the ceiling. Soon I could hear she was asleep. Apart from the slow rhythm of her breathing, the room was silent. I switched off the light. Somewhere outside, beyond the blind, a woman called out in Arabic. Like a squirt of oil on water, the sound of her voice curled slowly in my head.

23

The next day Anna and I ventured into the Fez *medina*. Needing a guide, we hired one from the tourist office and were soon in the maze, being swept behind his bobbing head like flotsam down a river of people. Flattening ourselves against walls to avoid laden donkeys, we spiralled onwards down dark alleys and into the guts of the labyrinth. From time to time the guide spoke to a stallholder before pointing at an article of merchandise and urging us to buy it. On each occasion, we enthused but declined.

'But what you want?' he asked exasperatedly.

'*Majoun*,' said Anna suddenly. Meaning, I soon discovered, cannabis jam. Her eyes were bright. 'Can you get it?'

The guide shook his head in a charade of dejection. 'Police,' he said, and rolled his eyes heavenwards in horror at the danger of it all.

'That's okay,' said Anna. 'We'll get it in Marrakesh.'

'Give me money,' said the guide. They bartered briefly before Anna lifted her jersey, removed several notes from a pouch strapped to her stomach and handed them to him.

'You wait here,' he said and vanished into the crush. Anna and I found a nook and waited. Remarkably, the guide soon returned. 'Good *majoun*,' he said and handed over a small package wrapped in paper.

On our way out of the *medina*, Anna was persuaded to have her feet decorated with henna. In a dark room an old Berber woman licked and stroked inky patterns around her toes and along her insteps with a fine brush. The lightness of the woman's touch set Anna's eyelids drooping and I too felt the gooseflesh of peacefulness at the intricacy of the designs that slowly emerged.

Later, back in the *ville nouvelle*, we bought a loaf from a *patisserie*. Back in our hotel room, we locked the door and Anna cut the bread with a penknife while I removed several fuel tablets from my backpack and boiled a dixie of water. With the weak black tea made, she passed me slices spread with *majoun* and we ate and drank in the leaden glare of the single bulb. The *majoun* tasted dusty and I settled for several slices while she had as many again.

'It takes time to work,' she said once we had finished. 'Let's have a bath and get ready.'

Again using bedroom mats as stepping stones on the flooded bathroom floor, Anna and I bathed together, she sitting crossways with her hennaed feet over the side while I lay full-length in the water, one leg behind her haunches and the other beneath her raised thighs. Because the awkwardness of her posture prevented her from washing easily, I did the soaping and sponging. As always, the sight and touch of her nakedness brought on tumescence but we restrained ourselves, wanting the *majoun* to act first.

After our bath I brewed more tea and we lay on our sleeping bags and sipped and waited.

'Nobody knows we're here, do they?' asked Anna suddenly.

'No,' I said. 'I'm lost and you're still at Cambridge.'

Feeling no effects of the *majoun*, I lay back and thought once again about the home I had left. About Sally, always cool and lithe in the summer heat. About Will; was he still alive? About the dogs and the cows and whether more farmers in the district had been murdered. Then I must have dozed off.

Some time later, I heard sounds in the bathroom – a person moving about clumsily and water running. I realised that something was happening when I felt myself levitating. At first it was comical but the more I tried to expel the notion of weightlessness, the more I felt suspended. Then the water stopped running and I could hear babbling and splashing. Suddenly the tenor of the sounds changed, becoming wildly agitated: yelps and moans and weeping. I closed my eyes and willed myself awake. When I came partly to my senses I was half out of my unzipped sleeping bag on the bed.

The noises in the bathroom had stopped but as I swung my legs onto the floor, Anna burst from the door. 'Where's the penknife?' she demanded, rummaging in my backpack. When she found nothing, she fell back on the bed, sobbing.

'What's the problem?' I heard my voice asking.

Anna dissolved in a paroxysm of weeping, then began kicking her legs and screamed: 'The mud's burning!' She fell forward onto the floor and tore at her insteps with her nails.

I stumbled forward and grasped her feet and hung onto them until she stopped kicking. At first it was all inexplicable but as my rationality returned, I began to puzzle out what was happening. Dredging an image from deep in Anna's past, the *majoun* had heated the henna patterns into geyser mud, a deduction she later confirmed.

Someone hammered on the wall from an adjoining room. 'It's all right,' I shouted.

Anna tried to sit up but I held her and we fell sideways onto the bed and lay in each others' arms, her jagged breathing snagging. 'Sleep,' I said, mouthing the word softly in her ear as I had done to Sally in Lamu after her nightmare about Alice. I unzipped a sleeping bag and placed it over her. She subsided slowly.

When she began breathing deeply and rhythmically, I wet a handkerchief with warm water and dabbed the seeping lacerations on her feet. The effort exhausted me so I switched off the light and lay down beside her, clasping her around the waist. Moonlight sliced through the blinds, ribbing the bed.

Later that night I had the strangest dream. I was out on a plain, somewhere in Africa. To my right was a multitude of blacks, to my left a multitude of whites, all clapping and gesticulating in slow-motion silence. In open ground in the centre was a girl, clearly Alice, running slowly and weightlessly down the corridor between the two groups. Her expression was blissful but she was vacillating, weaving between the imploring options, all veiled in silence.

I awoke in a state of anxiety, unsure what to make of it. Was it merely a clip of clichéd footage that my subconscious had worthlessly thrown up, or were there archetypal messages? I put it to Alice in my journal, hoping for an answer.

24

That was it. Thanks to the *majoun*, Fez was finished. Early next morning, Anna and I packed our bags and set off again, taking the train to Meknes and a succession of buses and taxis to the sacred town of Moulay Idriss and the Roman ruins at Volubilis. The countryside was beautiful, the tilled plains unrolling southwards towards the cedared slopes of the Middle Atlas.

While the *majoun* incident was irrelevant as a confession to Sally, it certainly had lessons for Alice and, like a diligent parent, I related a version to her. What Anna made of it, I don't know; we never discussed it and I didn't sneak a look at her journal. Reading Sally's notes had been harrowing enough and the last thing I needed was to once again discover disparaging comments about myself.

To begin with, Anna was strangely withdrawn, but as the train neared Meknes she burst into chatter. 'My Mum and Dad still think I'm at Cambridge,' she said breathlessly, having forgotten our conversation the previous evening. 'What if they've been trying to contact me? Nobody could tell them where I am.'

'Phone from Marrakesh,' I ventured. 'It'll be okay.'

But Anna's rising guilt had rekindled my usual anxieties. What if Sally were distraught and Will ailing and wanting to say goodbye? And what if the farm had been attacked now that I wasn't there to defend it? All the old questions begged answers which I couldn't provide.

Like Lamu, Moulay Idriss looks Grecian at first. It is a swarm of white-washed buildings around the tomb of its namesake, some Moroccan potentate from the past. Leaving the taxi in the square, we followed a guide up the hillside to a point from where photographs could be taken of the vista of the town. Progress was slow because Anna stopped frequently, complaining that her feet were hurting.

While I sat on a low wall and viewed the panorama, Anna took several snaps. Beside us on the steep hillside were humble shacks surrounded by areas of swept earth and fringes of litter in which lean-looking chickens were scratching. Moroccan peasant dwellings, I noted, are not unlike their South African counterparts. But back home, the condition of wretchedness seemed more loaded with menace. As the recession deepened and political transition hamstrung the police and army, so yells for retribution echoed from similar huts throughout South Africa and sent dishevelled *rastamen* deep into the forests from where they could watch the lights of white comfort and weigh up their options.

Wanting to return to Meknes by evening, we moved on to nearby Volubilis. Once the thriving capital of the Roman Empire's most southerly province, the city was the home of Cleopatra's daughter, something that caught Anna's fancy and had her asking questions of the toothless caretaker who seemed uncomprehending, muttering in Arabic and shaking his head.

Today Volubilis is an extensive grid of ruins on a fertile plain. No sooner had we begun to walk along the pathways than I found myself marvelling at the precision of its planning and the smallness of what was once a Roman provincial capital. Anna wandered ahead while I traced tenuous parallels between Imperial Rome and the old apartheid order. Both were mighty and repressive: one long in ruins and the other soon to follow.

What, I wondered, gave the Romans the confidence to build a city – with mansions, palaces, temples, baths, triumphal arch, olive presses, aqueducts and fountains – so far from home? I cast my musings further. What is it that grants confidence and then withdraws it? Even the intricacy of the mosaics attested to a conviction of immortality – a feeling so at odds with the farm where Sally and Will must be braced for expropriation. It is the same game played again and again: giving and taking. Using old scores to create new hurts.

The parallels were so close. As we picked our way through the mounds of masonry, I saw the symbols of the conqueror, like Afrikanerdom's Voortrekker Monument and Blood River laager – loved by some, hated by many, and soon to be overtaken by history.

We spent that night in Meknes. We found a bar in the city centre that sold beer and *brochettes*, and then turned in early in anticipation of our journey to Marrakesh.

How suddenly Anna had changed! No longer the footloose romantic, happy to drift through a Moroccan dream, she was now hesitant and anxious. Decisions had become dilemmas. Should she continue to Marrakesh or Casablanca? After all, both cities were merely names she wanted to say she had visited. Shouldn't she rather phone home immediately, confess her academic failure and take the shortest route back to New Zealand? In other words, the prodigal daughter option.

'No, Anna, you must see Marrakesh.' I was emphatic, playing for time.

But I never elaborated and Anna never asked. Anyway, I was a biased adviser. I needed Anna as much as I needed Marrakesh. I had conjured the city into the crossroads where the Arab north meets the heart of the continent, below which Southern Africa dangles like a sack of viscera. Somehow, in my mind, the High Atlas was a watershed: the serrated peaks sawing my idea of Africa into two portions: home and half-home. But by then I was so confused by what constituted belonging that anywhere with the right trappings could have been made into a refuge. However, it was more than that. I wanted Anna to stay because I thought her beautiful. And I was flattered that she depended on me.

I also needed a cultural buffer to keep Morocco at bay – someone who spoke the same language, literally and metaphorically. But, more importantly, my whole odyssey needed assurance. Otherwise, I was merely one of those fools who had fled their homeland and embarked on a journey to nowhere. Like Alice, perhaps.

25

How do I tell a tale to a girl of sixteen, especially one who may be dead? Do I merely relate it straight but omit words that could be difficult for a teenager? Or is it a more complex exercise, requiring sensitivity to the age gap and other differences? Also, can I qualify my statements or offer advice? In other words, can I put my own spin on things? This I certainly do in my confessions to Sally, which are full of artifice, but Alice is different. There is no baggage in her case; she is just a girl who disappeared. While the ripples she caused may have sunk my relationship with Sally, she was never blameworthy. Sally was. That's the distinction.

What follows is the real account of my departure from Morocco. It is reportage, not comment. My journal contains the other versions, each tailored to its own confessor, but they are another story.

Having skirted Rabat and Casablanca, our train swung south-eastwards into the desert. As we gunned over the sandy flatlands, so the colours changed: the gentle pastels of the coast washed into ochre and reddened as we neared Marrakesh. Images come to mind: herdboys tending sheep in grassless fields hedged with cacti; pylons, like ranks of forgotten scaffolding, throwing their mantis silhouettes across the sand; and lorries scurrying like beetles along the highway that runs parallel to the railway line.

Marrakesh. Anna and I repeated the word to each other as we pointed through the glass at the straggle of palms. Marrakesh. The magic of the name lifted our spirits. The threshold of the real Africa, said the guidebook. Beyond the city rose the peaks of the High Atlas, white and crisp with winter snow.

Soon we were there, in the low pink city with its avenues of orange trees. If our Moroccan run-around had been winding down since Anna's brush with the *majoun*, it gathered momentum after we emerged from the station and its hustlers and caught a taxi to the *medina*. As we swept down wide avenues, Anna was bright-eyed. 'Marrakesh!' she exclaimed, looking around her in wonderment.

How we loved the name then!

Through the open window I could smell the dust of home. Using spurious meteorology, I had it thrust upwards by the Drakensberg, swirled above the Great Lakes and the equator, and then eddied over the Sahara and High Atlas and into the dusty oasis. We chose a hotel in the *medina*. Nearby was the Djemaa el Fna, or Place of the Dead, an open area cluttered with stalls. No sooner had we left our luggage in the room than we rushed outside to watch the snake charmers, acrobats and others ply their trade.

It was exhaustingly frenetic. After moving from stall to stall, handling trinkets and haggling, we escaped through a dingy cafe to a rooftop terrace where the spectacle could be viewed from a distance. There we sat for the remainder of the afternoon, drinking mint tea and writing up our journals.

At dusk we returned to the hotel, showered and went downstairs to eat in the dining room. A variety of meat dishes and mounds of couscous lined one wall as we sat at low tables and an elderly man wearing a bright *djellaba* played a mandolin and sang mournfully.

Afterwards, Anna went outside to a public callbox to phone home. Meanwhile, I sat in the room, paging through the travel guide, but my thoughts had returned to the paddocks with the duikers picking their way daintily through the peach trees and the cows standing in the dappled shade, only their jaws moving and their tails flicking at flies. Beyond the rye grass fields, I could hear the cries of hadedahs, their stridency softened by distance. And, at the house, I saw Will dozing in a deck chair on the verandah while Sally sunbathed on the lawn, her eyes closed and her hair shining.

Presently, Anna returned, ebullient. 'My parents freaked when I said I'd left Cambridge. And when I told them I was in Marrakesh they nearly died. But I said nice things about you. They want me to come home. My Dad's going to book me a flight. He's going to phone the hotel tomorrow evening.'

It was as I had imagined, but the flight booking sounded brutally final. The prospect of Anna leaving devastated me, but I said nothing. I had become resigned to travelling alone. Anyway, I had survived the loss of Sally so could manage the loss of Anna too. All that was left was for us was to have fun together as our time ran out.

We spent the next day in the *souks*. As usual, hustlers hounded us, touting for custom and ignoring our polite refusals. And yet again one persisted, whom we did our best to parry gently. But when he began to tug at Anna's shirt, I touched him on the chest and told him firmly to leave us alone. At this he exploded in feigned anger, vilifying us loudly to passersby and shouting for a policeman.

'Let's go,' said Anna seconds before I lashed out, and she dragged me away to the rooftop terrace.

That evening, as promised, Anna's father phoned. She was to fly from Casablanca the day after next. We planned to leave Marrakesh the following morning but were advised against it by an Australian we met at supper. 'Stay here,' he said, gold rings in his ears, and his beard bleached by the sun. 'Casablanca's modern and up to shit. Have you visited the Gardens of Menara?'

'No,' we said.

'Then you must,' he urged. 'They're beautiful.'

And so our penultimate day was spent in Marrakesh, not Casablanca. We never saw the Australian again, but his advice was to have momentous consequences. In the same way as when I met Andrew Trevelyn on the Cambridge train, my life took an unexpected turn. Once again it was brought home to me that it is only time and place that count. You move towards trouble or stand still and have it come to you.

Before bed that night we went up onto the roof of our hotel, finding several deck chairs beside the washing lines. Below us was the Djemaa el Fna, the stallholders' gaslights shining in the dark. In line with our established ritual, Anna produced a joint and we smoked it, listening to the thudding of drums in the square and the nasal sonar of cats along the rooftops. Looking south-eastwards, I visualised the silent peaks of the High Atlas, each icy with snow. I thought also of the Africa beyond, its foreignness and familiarity. As the night deepened, a chill breeze stirred the washing lines, nudging Anna and me into each others' arms. It was slow and cold and quiet.

26

En route to the gardens next morning, we passed the Hotel Mamounia. Now plush and modern, it is a mecca for wealthy tourists. But earlier this century, when it was old and gracious, it was apparently Winston Churchill's favourite hotel in the world. He visited it often, sitting in the garden and painting panoramas backed by the High Atlas. Like Matisse in Tangier, Churchill in later life sought Africa from the refuge of a hotel garden. It is a stratagem I can understand.

As an indication of how much Anna's spirits had lifted, she never once complained about the cuts on her ankles during our stay in Marrakesh. There was even a bounce in her step that morning as we strolled through the Menara gate and between the rows of olive trees.

In the centre of the gardens was a large reservoir with a pink summer pavilion beside it, and palms and cypresses, all backed by the ubiquitous High Atlas with its mantle of snow. So still was the water's surface that the entire vista was caught in its mirror. Entranced, we stared at the twin pavilions issuing from the water's edge, the cypresses duplicated into moustaches and the palms into dumbbells, all enclosed by white serrations.

But our reverie was short-lived. Up steps around the reservoir advanced several hustlers armed with curios. And with their persistent entreaties and snatching fingers, they soon had Anna and me back on the defensive. The few other tourists there with us were also accosted and forced to barter.

One of the men had a tray of Berber earrings and necklaces that he thrust under Anna's face. And it was then that she made her mistake. A necklace intrigued her and she enquired about its price.

'Three hundred *dirhams*,' said the man, at which I laughed.

After a bout of haggling, Anna wavered, unzipping her money pouch and counting out several notes before deciding against buying.

'It's very nice,' she said to the man, lifting the necklace and holding it to her chest. 'But your price is still too high.'

Seemingly unperturbed, the hustler followed us around the reservoir making counter-offers. When Anna didn't respond, he said: 'I have more necklaces down the steps. Come.'

We followed. The other tourists were on the opposite side of the reservoir, talking loudly and taking photographs.

Once we were down the steps and beside the retaining wall, the man pulled a cloth bag from behind a shrub and beckoned Anna. She moved to him and leaned forward to look inside while he held it open. Then, blindingly fast, he grabbed her around the neck and held a knife to her throat.

'Give me your money,' he demanded, 'or I stick the girl.'

Pulling open my jacket and shirt, I removed all the *dirham* notes from my money pouch and offered them to him.

'In the bag,' he said, indicating.

I nodded. Anna's eyes were wide, the blade nestling against the softness of her neck.

As I leant to put the money in the bag, I saw my chance and lunged forward, slamming a fist in his stomach with all my strength and snatching for the knife with my other hand. Miraculously, my punch struck home, sinking deep into his guts. As he doubled up he slashed at me while Anna broke loose, spinning aside and stumbling into the shrubbery. Focusing on the knife, I grabbed his wrist with both hands and kicked him hard in the balls. Once again it worked. He toppled forward onto his knees like a devotee at confession. I then brought my knee up into his face. As his head snapped back, the knife spun from his hand and he slumped forward onto his stomach.

It all took only seconds. At that point Anna and I should have run away, but we didn't. While Anna sat among the foliage, I spun into a fearsome overdrive, kicking the fallen man repeatedly in the head and torso. It wasn't the first time I had done something like this. Ten years earlier, after a firefight in the Angolan bush, with our dead strewn among the undergrowth, those of us who had survived had done the same to the enemy wounded before dispatching them with shots to the head. But as I have a stomach only for maiming, I left the coups de grace to others.

I continued my frenzied assault until Anna lurched from the

shrubbery and screamed at me to stop. But I was beyond hearing. She then grabbed me by the arm and dragged me aside. The man lay motionless with blood trickling from his nose onto the sand.

With Anna leading, we headed back through the olive trees. Miraculously, it seemed no-one had seen the fight but we both knew the body would soon be found and the alarm raised. 'Be calm,' I repeated to myself silently. Holding back, we walked as normally as possible to the gate and flagged down a horse and trap. Once aboard, Anna and I held hands tightly to stop our trembling.

As soon as we were back in our hotel room, Anna gabbled: 'You may have killed him. We must leave now.'

'Yes,' I said.

We packed feverishly. I then went downstairs to the reception desk and settled the bill, saying we had to leave unexpectedly for Quarzazate, on the edge of the Sahara, leaving a false lead in case we were followed. Also to hide our tracks, instead of taking a taxi from outside the hotel we crossed the Djemaa el Fna and took one in the warren of streets behind it. Luckily, we reached the station only minutes before a train left for Casablanca and were soon aboard and slicing through the desert. Behind us, the low, pink skyline with its towering minaret and pattern of palms, backed by the snowy ramparts of the High Atlas, sank into the sand.

'We should have gone to the police and explained everything,' said Anna.

'Yes,' I said, 'ideally. But if he's dead, what makes you think they'll believe our story? And if he isn't dead, it'll be his word against ours. And remember, I'm a white South African. On a charge of murder or assault, you don't really think I'll get a fair hearing in Africa?'

We reached Casablanca late in the afternoon. Once again we took precautions. Rather than choose a taxi from the rank outside the station, we used the guidebook as a map and lugged our backpacks to the Hotel Excelsior.

'So this is Casablanca,' said Anna. 'It's so art deco.'

'It's like Durban,' I said. 'Even Mombasa. It has the same coastal feel.'

Before we reached the hotel, we made a plan. Assuming receptionists to be police informers, we decided that Anna should go in alone and take a single room while I waited nearby at a pavement

132

café. Once she had checked in and had her luggage taken upstairs, she would ostensibly go for a stroll but meet me outside. All this we did, finding a cheapish restaurant for our last supper. Later, we returned to the hotel as planned. While Anna distracted the receptionist, I slipped through the foyer and up the stairs.

What the Hotel Villa de France once was to Tangier, so the Excelsior had been Casablanca's grand hotel. Its elegant proportions were redolent of a past era of French confidence and style. Sneaking down a wide passage, we locked ourselves in our room and opened the shutters. Below was the *medina*, full of sweet-and-sour allure. Anna wrote several postcards to Cambridge friends, wanting to make use of the Casablanca date stamp. Then, conscious that our time together was slipping away, we bathed and lay down beside each other on the bed. Anna had a clean soap smell and her hair was loose and flowing.

In the glow sifting through the shutters, we began to make love. At first our tempo was slow and languorous but we soon climbed sharply, teetered and fell. (I made much of this in my confession to Sally.) Afterwards, as we lay together, I had a dam-burst of childhood memories and associations, the saltiness of Casablanca's air recalling Natal's coastline: waves scooting up beaches and boiling in retreat, rockpools with their swaying filigree and darting fingerlings, sand dunes ribbed with *strandloper* shells. And stays at Durban's Royal Hotel with my parents spawned images of coolness in the palm court but shimmering dampness in the street outside. Through the window I watched pigeons strutting and bobbing on the war memorial in the gardens beside the city hall, and people lolling on the lawns where I later imagined mounds of corpses.

'What will you do when I'm gone?' Anna asked, snapping on the bedside light but keeping her eyes closed.

'Head back to Europe,' I said. 'Probably Spain or Portugal.'

'What about Gibraltar?' she asked. 'It's English.'

'Maybe. I'll get to Tangier and see.'

'You'd better not take the train. It'll be too easy for them to catch you if they're on our trail.'

'I'll take a bus on a roundabout route,' I said. And I opened the guidebook and we plotted an arc south-eastwards into the Middle Atlas and then northwards via the Rif to Tangier. 'It's been fun,' Anna said.

'Yes,' I replied. 'It's been great.'

'You must let me know where you end up.'

'Sure,' I said.

We pulled up the blankets and fell asleep in each other's arms. But I had a restless night, pursued by the bloodied hustler and watched by a young blonde woman standing motionless on a road in a desert.

27

With Anna's flight scheduled for mid-morning, we rose early and repeated our diversionary tactics to get me out of the hotel. Once outside, we found a coffee shop for a snack and then ducked down a side-street to the bus station. Paranoid that the security net would close at the airport, we decided to part ways. Our reasoning was simple: if they were looking for a Bonnie and Clyde, we each stood a better chance alone. While Anna jetted out unnoticed, I would jink through the hinterland.

So, amidst the bustle of the terminus, we embraced tightly. Anna cried a little and I had to fight back tears. She then climbed on the coach and we waved at each other until she rounded a corner and was gone.

Feeling utterly alone, I found a bus headed for the Middle Atlas. And so began a journey along a thread of roads that strung together places called Khourigba, Kasba-Tadla, Khenifra, Azrou, Guercif, Oujda, Ketama, Chaouen and Tetouan before Tangier's white Legoland unfolded from the foothills, with the blue band of the Mediterranean gleaming beyond it.

Once back on the promenade, among the veiled women and the men in their *djellabas*, I headed up the hillside to the Hotel El Muniria.

'So you've lost the girl,' said the proprietor.

'Do you have a room?' I asked.

He gave me number nine, where Burroughs had written *The Naked Lunch*. Remembering how much that literary association had excited Anna, I took the offer as a good omen. But if the book is a glimpse of hell, as Anna had explained, then I visited it that night in my dreams.

Finding the young Arab barman alone in the bar the following morning, I told him my passport had been stolen and that I wanted to be smuggled to Gibraltar.

'You see, I am a South African,' I added. 'It's hard for me to get another passport. And I don't want any problems with the police.'

'I will find out,' he said. 'I will tell you this evening.'

Rather than retrace our steps of the previous month and wallow in nostalgia, I spent the day either in my room or sitting in the sun on the rooftop outside my window. Beyond the Tangerine skyline with its skeins of laundry, boats nosed into the Mediterranean and gulls wheeled like the egrets did when I ploughed the rye-grass fields back home.

Late in the afternoon, the barman tapped on my door. 'You will go tonight,' he said. 'Someone will come at ten o'clock. I will call you.'

'How much?' I asked.

'Six hundred *dirhams*.'

When I raised my eyebrows, he added: 'It is a fixed price.'

'Can I trust these people?' I asked. The barman nodded. 'I have friends in Gibraltar,' I lied. 'I will phone them to say that if I have not arrived there by tomorrow night, they must come and find you here.'

'Okay,' he said.

My courier was punctual. A youth with a wall-eye, he led me along a succession of alleys in the direction of the Grand Socco. Eventually we reached a waiting car that took us to a house beneath the crenellated heights of the kasbah before doubling back through the *ville nouvelle* and into the countryside. After some time, we stopped on a road flanked by tall palms. When I climbed out of the car, I could hear waves. The boy beckoned and I followed him as the car turned and headed back towards Tangier, its tail-lights glowing in the dark.

Some minutes later we reached a shack where I was given a glass of mint tea by a Berber woman with facial tattoos. The boy signalled for me to wait and disappeared. The light was bad and I remember hearing women's voices in an adjoining room. Some time later the boy returned with a bearded man who asked in French for money, rubbing together his thumb and index finger. I looked at the youth. He nodded. Apprehensively, I handed over the notes.

'Come,' said the man in French and I followed him outside and along a footpath through the darkness. This is it, I told myself: a blow to the head and no-one would miss me. Even Anna wouldn't know, merely assuming that I had reneged on our agreement to keep in touch. My only comeback would be the El Muniria barman, but if I didn't survive there would be no-one to confront him.

Presently we came to a beach and I was led through the shallows to a boat. There was little moonlight and all I could see was a dark shape against which water was lapping and sucking. I was helped aboard and into the hold where several other people were huddled. Because they were wrapped in shawls and blankets, I never saw their faces but assumed that like me, they were Africans hoping to infiltrate Europe. A diesel engine started and at low revs we edged seawards, our noise drowned by the rush of the surf.

Luckily the sea was calm as we nosed out into the strait. The air in the hold was so foetid that I climbed up on deck and sat on a box as the dark water sluiced by and several shadowy crewmen went about their duties. On two occasions, tankers passed, their superstructures studded with lights and their bows as sharp as axe-heads in the night.

As on my trip out from Algeciras, I became acutely conscious of the strange ambiguities of my Euro-Africanness. Although hugely relieved to be escaping from what I had come to imagine as decades in a Moroccan jail, I was equally aware that for expatriates like myself there is no escape. The dim memories of my childhood at a trading store in Zululand, the horror of my parents' murder while I was away at boarding school, the messy skirmishes in the Angolan bush, are baggage I cannot jettison. Neither can I throw aside the kindness of Will and Sally who gave me refuge for five years before Alice Walker disappeared and things fell apart. I often berate myself for leaving but it is hard to be rational in the face of betrayal. For better or worse, I am what I am and must press onwards in the only manner I know how.

And so we tacked through the darkness, tugged by cross-currents and passing lights to our left before the captain decelerated, edging the boat forwards until the sound of the surf could be heard above the slow thump of the engine. The other passengers filed up on deck, secretive figures swathed in blankets.

The captain spoke quietly, gesticulating for us to wade ashore as the boat rose and fell, its engine throbbing. 'Gibraltar,' he said, pointing to a hill of lights in the distance.

Holding my backpack above my head, I eased myself over the

side and sank up to my chest in the water. Then, labouring to keep my balance against the swell, I waded ashore. No sooner had I reached the Spanish beach than the boat was gone and the other passengers were dispersing in the darkness. I headed inland, knowing I had a better chance masquerading as a European backpacker than sticking with my fellow Africans who were so conspicuously alien.

After walking for half an hour, skirting any habitation for fear of dogs, I found a stone wall and lay down beside it in a bower of undergrowth. Dozing until dawn, I then peered out of my refuge and saw the Rock some distance to the south. It immediately struck me that the towering sphinx-like shape was a larger, blunter version of Isandlwana, the hill in Zululand where the British were so ignominiously defeated by the Zulus late last century. Having spent my childhood near that killing field, I found the resemblance reassuring.

Breaking cover, I walked confidently across several fields until I found a road leading to the village of San Roque. From there I caught a bus to the terminus at La Linea, and then walked to the checkpoint below the Rock. Barely looking up from the magazine he was reading, the Spanish official waved me through. Next, the young bobby on duty glanced at my South African passport and asked: 'What's the purpose of your visit to Gibraltar? How long do you intend to stay?'

'Just to see the place,' I said. 'A couple of days.'

He nodded, not even bothering to stamp my papers. I strode out onto the runway that crosses the isthmus on the British side. Above me loomed the limestone cliffs of the Rock. High on the slopes, a Union Jack flapped from the battlements of a Moorish castle. I strode off towards the town.

PART THREE
The Rock

28

So here I am in Gibraltar. I board with a Mrs Olive Rook on Engineer Road, not far from the cable car that takes tourists from the town to the top of the Rock. From my window I have a wide view of the bay, across the naval craft to Algericas and the distant arc of the Spanish coastline. When the weather is clear, I can see Africa – a brooding presence on the horizon.

Mrs Rook is an army widow who supplements her pension by taking a lodger. Small and bustling, she is a model of niceness. Her sitting-room is a shrine to the memory of her husband: *kukris*, badges and regimental photographs. With my father having fought in Korea, and having seen action myself in the South African Army, I pass Mrs Rook's test of militariness. This strengthens our kinship immeasurably. We talk, she says, the same language. We tell each other stories over tea and Jaffa cakes, she about camp life in the East, me about firefights with MPLA and Cuban troops in the Angolan bush. These sessions give us both pleasure. She tells a good story and I invigorate myself by romanticising those days when life jostled with death. We never moralise, just remember. We have what could be called a symbiotic relationship.

She frequently asks me about Africa and I tell her what I can. We talk of Morocco, which she sees from her window but has never visited, and of Kenya and Angola. And, naturally, of South Africa. 'Your old home' she calls it. I tell her everything but leave certain things out, if you know what I mean. She knows of the farm and my life with Sally, and even something about Alice Walker's disappearance. But I have also manipulated facts. For example, I have told her my reason for leaving was Sally's death. It's not true, of course, but it's easier than explaining the implications of Alice's lostness and Sally's fateful involvement in the affair. So I fudge it all, having Sally die in a car accident and Alice merely run away. These, I tell Mrs Rook, are the reasons for my odyssey. I had to put it all behind me.

'But why Gibraltar?' she asks.

'I don't know, Mrs Rook.'

'Come on, Christopher Jameson,' she admonishes me gently, 'you must have a reason.'

'I came and liked it here, Mrs Rook,' I reply with complete honesty. 'I saw some of Europe and went back to Africa but got tired of the place again. So I wanted to find somewhere that was in-between.'

'You're dead right, she says, clapping her hands. 'Gibraltar's just like that.'

Mrs Rook is canny. She's got an inkling of what it's all about. In fact, she's clearer on the domicile issue than I am. But what she doesn't know is the main reason I've spent the last eleven months in Gibraltar. She has no idea that I like it here because the future is so uncertain. I need the doubt as much as I hate it. The more Spain demands this rocky appendix, and the more Britain wavers, the greater the boost to that nagging dynamo deep in my head. My machine that runs on uncertainty, the one that powers me.

With Morocco having swallowed what was left of my funds, I have rejoined the job market. Since just after my arrival in Gibraltar, I have worked in a pub near the Convent, the governor's residence. The clientele is mixed – soldiers, sailors, artisans, businessmen – and I have come to like them. Without the necessary documentation to stay here, though, I fully expect to be picked up by the police, but so far so good.

Mrs Rook says she has contacts and has promised to put in a good word for me if the need arises. Except perhaps for the Spaniards, all of us know we are living on borrowed time. What the hell? seems the general feeling. As I have said, that's the main reason I like it here.

Working in the pub in the evenings brings in enough to live on. I can square up with Mrs Rook and buy necessities from the Safeways supermarket in Main Street. To supplement this, I sometimes help in the cinema behind the Queen's Hotel. I don't do much except ensure that the takings are safe and the crowd behaves. Whenever kids get carried away I tell them off politely and they listen. Occasionally, some yob answers me back and I have to suppress that urge for mayhem. So far I haven't reached boiling point. But that time, I suppose, will come.

I have also been putting aside a bit each month. Although my savings are modest, they're rising slowly and soon I'll have enough to spread my wings. Even fly back to South Africa, if I want to. Failing that, I can choose another destination and head off in search of greener pastures. But, for now, Gibraltar's fine.

After work each evening, I stroll along Main Street, through the Southport Gates, past the Trafalgar Cemetery, and diagonally up the side of the Rock, letting myself quietly into the house. Mrs Rook is asleep and I can hear her breathing as I tiptoe along the passage. Every night I make myself a cup of tea in the kitchen and then lie on my bed and read the *Gibraltar Chronicle* or scribble notes for this book you're reading. The writing bit is very difficult but it helps me get things into perspective. Daily, I relive more of the last two years and as my memories settle so I understand better how Alice Walker's disappearance set me on a long and winding road to this small room in this forgotten outpost. It's a strange and compelling story. At least I think so.

Also, I have a love interest. Jill works in The Rock and Keys with me, pulling pints of bitter and pushing tumblers up under the inverted spirit bottles like calves nudging udders for milk. Born in Nairobi the night before Kenya's independence, she's another service widow. Her husband was killed in action with the Paras at Goose Green during the Falklands campaign. We see each other every evening, except on my night off when I either help out at the cinema or stay at home with Mrs Rook watching television and talking. The story's simple: somehow Jill ended up on the Rock and somehow we ended up together. It's a frank relationship. Whenever we feel the urge, we retire to her flat at closing time for a scrum – that's what she calls it.

Mrs Rook and Jill are also fond of each other and sometimes we go on picnics together like a family – either to the Alameda Gardens, just below Engineer Road, or more often to the apes at Queens Gate on the Rock itself. Although tail-less, the apes are not unlike the vervet monkeys back in Natal. They are a sprightly troop that keep us amused with their antics. When the weather's clear and we're on the Rock, I can't help staring at Africa in the distance. Like the apes, I come from there. After I came from Europe, of course.

On my days off I take much the same routes, either walking up the Rock to enjoy the company of my kinfolk and the sweeping view of the African coastline or wandering through the Gardens with its wealth of familiar flora. It's hugely reassuring to note how well many African trees and shrubs have transplanted. There's hope for us all.

Seeing those plants which I associate with my sub-tropical childhood also helps me dredge from within myself later snippets that I include in these memoirs. In fact, drawing on such associations is almost as rich a source as Sally's diaries. You will remember, I stole them from among her underwear in her cupboard when I made my anguished retreat from that other life just over a year ago.

As I reread the scribbled pages I learn a lot about Sally and myself. I can see the withdrawn young farmer who exasperated her so: the young man absorbed by the production and welfare of his cows and the vigour of his fodder crops; the young man apparently unaffected by the anarchy spreading through the country. How misleading appearances can be! Or how inaccurate are the images we project, even to our loved ones. That I was as concerned as Sally about the poverty and lawlessness escaped her. That I was also seeking equality and a place in the sun for all seems also to have gone unnoticed. Whose fault was my predicament? Mine, hers or Alice's for vanishing and changing the whole picture?

At times, with hindsight, my emotional departure from the farm seems an overreaction. I could just as easily have confronted Sally and thrashed the matter out. Even if things were irreconcilable, I could have claimed compensation for my years of contribution and gone my separate way. Despite the violence and uncertainty, there must have been a demand for reliable agricultural help. I could even have tried Zimbabwe or Zambia.

But it was more than that; I had to get away from it all. Politics, politics, politics. It wears you down in the end. One has only so much room for accusations and counter-accusations. And then one gags on them and has to go.

It's New Year's Eve tomorrow – a year since my wanderings in Spain before my departure for Morocco. Things have cheered up in the last twelve months. Although dear Anna's gone, I've still got Jill. In fact, all in all, this memoir may give the impression that I'm something of a womaniser: Sally, Molly, Anna, Jill, even that tattooed senorita in Barcelona. But it's not true really; I'm not in search of conquests. I have my rising sap, of course, but I'm seeking more than physical release. What it is, I can't accurately describe. Foundness, I suppose. That's as good a description as any. Tomorrow night, Mrs Rook, Jill and I will attend a service in the cathedral to say goodbye to the old year. Then, it's on to the Rock Hotel for dinner. After eleven, we're planning to get a lift to the top of the Rock itself to watch the governor and chief minister light a bonfire at midnight. Gibraltar's beacon will be the most southerly among a thousand lit across Europe to symbolise a new era of unity and freedom among the countries of the continent. The idea, says Mrs Rook, is that each beacon will be visible from its neighbours, forming a chain of light in the darkness. It should be fun. Everyone will be expectant of the new year, wishing for the rejuvenation that is always hoped for but never comes. And far below us, at the bewitching hour, the ships in the harbour will begin their siren song and the drone will rise in the night, as if from deep within the Rock itself.

Outside, a wind is blowing, scouring the crags, agitating the shutters, and no doubt making the prows of the few warships in the docks heave slowly in the swell. I finish my mug of tea and pull up my sleeping-bag like an eiderdown. Then I switch off the light and lie snug in the darkness, the Rock behind me and across the sheet of inky water, the bulk of Africa, sleeping.

29

Since my arrival in Gibraltar, I've had two notable encounters concerning Alice, both in The Rock and Keys. On the first occasion, I got talking to a man who came in early one evening and sat drinking at the bar. A forensic entomologist, he was in Gibraltar for an inquiry into the death of a Spanish girl whose body had been found hidden on the Rock. Although it was clearly a case of sexual assault and murder, he had been brought in to determine the time of death. This was crucial because the two main suspects – a British soldier and a Moroccan fisherman – had alibis before or after certain dates. If he could pinpoint the day of the crime, the prosecution could home in on the suspect who was in town at the time.

Excited that he may throw new light on Alice, I asked Professor Walter Mason how he used insects to solve crimes. He gave a long explanation of how successive waves of bugs descend on a corpse and how the presence of this fly or that beetle tell the informed viewer all they need to know. 'Because,' he added, 'when the body dies it comes to life.' He smiled, the contradiction appealing to him.

'If it is hot and humid, as it was on the evening when Maria Benitez was raped and murdered, blowflies can arrive within half an hour of death.' He took a gulp of whisky. 'They then lay eggs and in a few days the corpse is alive with maggots.' Another contradiction; another smile.

'Because the life cycle of blowflies is very regular, the ages of eggs, maggots or pupae can be accurately estimated. Once this has been done, one takes into account environmental factors like temperature and humidity and works backwards to estimate the time of death. The police then marry that information with the whereabouts of the suspects and try and build a case.'

It was macabre, yet riveting. Juggling my duties, I hovered down his end of the counter as he told me about cases of murderers who were convinced they had committed the perfect crime being caught because flies' eggs could only have been laid before or after a particular date; and other instances where sentenced killers had been released from prison because entomological evidence indicated a time of death when they had an alibi. One example hinged on the fact that carrion flies are not active on cold winter evenings so the newly-hatched maggots noted in the autopsy could only have been laid on the corpse some time before dark. This meant that the murder must have taken place earlier in the day when the convicted man could prove he was not at the scene.

So he went on. And unlike much of this account of Alice and Sally and my flight to Europe and subsequent wanderings, it was only several hours old when I recorded it in my room later that evening. As I sat at my desk, the obvious occurred to me: there is no Alice corpse. And while we all hoped against hope that she was still alive, if she wasn't, her body must be found. Once that happened, someone like Walter Mason could be brought in to help solve the riddle. I became so enthusiastic that I immediately devised a plan to get the investigation going again. It was simple. I would write an anonymous note to Sally's editor saying that I knew where the corpse was. This should put the case back on the front page and, with luck, could throw up something of interest. After all, this was no different from the strategy Sally had adopted except that I would not make the mistake of pointing fingers at anyone. All I would be doing is saying: I know where it is, go and look, and if you don't find it, then keep looking.

So I found a sheet of paper and wrote:

Letters to the Editor, Natal Times
Dear Sir,

Who I am is not important, but I can tell you where Alice Walker is. Remember the girl who vanished in Gatacre Drive? Well, go to the piece of bush that runs down the hill near the drive. Follow the stream that runs down the bush to near where it flows past the playing fields of the primary school. There, under some big rocks. That's where she is. Or was.
Good luck.

Over the next few days I compiled a collage using separate letters cut from a copy of the *Daily Mail* which a client had left in the pub. It was finicky work and I had to borrow the tweezers Jill uses to pluck her eyebrows so that each letter could be brushed across the glue-stick and fixed to the page. Once the composite was completed, I photocopied it. The result was fair; the words were somewhat irregular but the message was clear.

However, the address on the envelope posed more of a problem. To create it from cut-outs would invite attention. Needing something commonplace, I contemplated using Mrs Rook's old typewriter on the afternoon she plays bridge at a friend's flat but decided against this because there must be so few of its vintage around any more that it would be easy to trace. Instead, after much deliberation, I made use of the computer printer in the office at the pub. One evening, knowing it would be my turn to lock up, I printed the address on the envelope in bold type, assuming that the darker the letters, the more difficult it would be to pick up any idiosyncracies of typeface.

As Mrs Rook was about to leave for her annual week-long visit to her daughter in Hove, I asked her to post the letter in London where she would be staying overnight before travelling to the coast. Because so many letters are sent to South Africa from Britain, mine would be one of thousands. I also told Mrs Rook that I wanted it posted in London rather than Gibraltar because it was a birthday note to a friend and needed to reach its destination in a hurry.

As an additional precaution, I addressed it to the librarian rather than the editor of the *Natal Times* because Sally had told me that the librarian is in charge of processing the editorial post. Remembering the name of the librarian Sally had mentioned before I left, I addressed it to her, being careful to provide only an initial and no honorific so that the gender of the writer would remain unspecific. I used only the newspaper's box number, city and country because its name and street were more likely to stick in the mind. The effect of this, I surmised, would be twofold: it would attract the least attention from the postal authorities but would tell the people on the paper that the writer was no crank and even had inside knowledge.

I also took precautions in my handling of the envelope, holding it by the edges and taking care not to allow my fingers or thumb to touch the front or back. This paranoia stemmed from my national service days when all combat troops had their fingerprints and dental records taken just in case they were blown to smithereens or incinerated and identification of the remains therefore became a problem. If they had my prints somewhere, there was always the chance that a government computer would link up the smudges on a tired envelope with the whorls on a troopie's thumb and I would be fingered.

If the letter was seen as more than a hoax and caused a fuss in Bushmansburg, then any publicity it may generate in Britain, given that letters take a week or so to reach South Africa, would probably occur after Mrs Rook had returned to Gibraltar. And as the only newspaper she read was the *Gibraltar Chronicle*, it was highly unlikely that she would connect a personal birthday greeting from her lodger to a friend in South Africa with a tip-off about a corpse in a *cause celèbre*.

Of course, I am making much out of almost nothing. I have no clue as to where Alice's body is, alive or dead, but if the clairvoyant feels she is in water, then what better place than downstream in the watercourse she had to cross if she took the short cut through the finger of bush to the Morgans or Jacksons? All I'm doing is following logic in the face of ignorance. And even if the police have searched that area many times, as I know they have, then in the light of nothing more definite they will do so again, understanding that sniffer dogs are not at their best around water and that they may have missed something. And even if they don't find anything which, but for a fluke, will be the case, they will say to themselves that the writer may be correct but that flashfloods, dogs, jackals and *goggas* of the kind in which Professor Mason specialises have all done their bit in reducing her to nothing.

Also, so much has happened in South Africa since I left that Alice may no longer be of any consequence. If the TV and newspapers are telling the true story, then with democracy has come transformation and the likes of Alice are no longer prize creatures deserving special treatment but ordinary citizens like all the rest. And with the escalating crime rate that has followed freedom, the police once again have far bigger fish to fry. Perhaps there is no longer an Alice file or, if there is, it is lying in a forgotten cabinet gathering dust.

30

The second encounter occurred several days ago, six weeks after my meeting with Professor Mason and a month after Mrs Rook posted my Alice letter in London to the *Natal Times* librarian. It also took place in the pub, at lunch, when a young couple entered and walked up to the bar. They were in their thirties, she slim and blonde and he compact and ruddy-faced. With their jeans and windbreakers and hiking shoes, they could only be travellers passing through.

'Two beers, please,' said the man. And he raised two fingers as if in a victory sign.

I started momentarily. His accent was unmistakable. 'You South African?' I enquired.

'Yes.' His tone was cautious.

'Where?'

'Natal.'

'Shake on it!' I exclaimed, extending a hand. 'I'm Chris.' The couple laughed. Her eyes were sparkling blue.

'John and Heather,' they said. We shook hands.

'Where in Natal?' I delved again.

'Near Nonoti on the north coast.'

'A sugar farm?'

'Yes. And you?'

'A dairy farm,' I said. 'Outside Bushmansburg.'

'Small world,' I laughed, pouring two pints of bitter and pushing the tankards across the counter. 'It's on me. Give me news.'

How we talked! As we dissected the familiar turf, me probing and them informing, I divided my attention between my duties and the exhilarating exchange: talking, nodding, pouring and working the till.

For an hour we plotted ourselves in terms of each other, sounding and rebounding our familiar code. They too were on the run, albeit only briefly. Drought was devastating Natal and they had fled from stunted and arrowing cane and the nightly flares of arson fires.

'Are you on two-way radio?' I asked, meaning the network that links farmers for protection; the one we had joined after Edward Mortimer's murder.

'Yes.'

'Have there been any attacks?'

'Plenty,' they replied. 'Every month some farmer gets hit.'

'But not us yet,' she smiled grimly, tapping the wooden counter.

'Do you ever go to Bushmansburg?' I asked.

'Only once a year for the agricultural show.'

'You don't know anyone called Sally Bowen?'

'No,' they said. 'Why?'

'Just a friend.' I paused. 'And have you heard of Alice Walker? The girl who disappeared?'

'Yes,' they said. 'A lot.'

'Have they found her?'

'No,' he said. 'But there's been news recently. The *Natal Times* has received a letter from the murderer, who is in London, telling them where the body is. They've looked but found nothing. The police are sure the letter's genuine but that there's just nothing left of Alice Walker any more. Interpol has been called in. They're hot on the murderer's trail.' He hesitated. 'Did you know her?'

'No, but it was big news when I left and I've always wondered what happened.'

'Why did you leave?' asked Heather.

'It's a long story. But, basically, my fiancée was killed and I wanted to get away. I travelled around, made a few friends and ended up here.'

They expressed their condolences and I accepted them with appropriate grace.

'Thanks,' I said. After a pause, I asked: 'Where were you last night?'

'We came down by train from Barcelona?'

'Ditto,' I said. 'A year ago I did the same. Was the compartment full?'

'Packed. We couldn't sleep.'

'Ditto,' I said. 'Where you headed?'

'Tangier.'

I laughed. 'You must be following me.' And I told them of the customs official on the ferry and the hustlers on the Tangerine waterfront. 'And, don't forget,' I added, 'it's Africa over there.'

'It can't be more dangerous than home,' they laughed. 'We'll be ready.'

But only once back in my room that night did I grasp the full impact of what they had said. Everyone was conning everyone. While I may have started the big ruse with my letter, Sally or Marais or some law-and-order worthy was using it to get themselves off the hook. After more than a year of uncertainty, the case was being honourably closed. Regrettably, Alice was no longer alive but the murderer had been traced to London and it was now all in the hands of Interpol. This had been kept secret for fear of jeopardising the investigations, but now that the murderer had chosen to communicate with the local press, the police felt able to acknowledge the truth.

I can see it clearly: the front-page report in the *Natal Times*, including a transcript of my letter and a photograph of Alice, as well as lengthy quotes from the police media liaison officer offering sympathies to the Walker family, and congratulating his team of detectives for being so hot on the killer's trail that they drove him from the country. Further, much would be made of how the investigation had been passed on to Interpol with whom the new South African Police Service is on the most cordial of terms. If it was as I thought, I had to hand it to the police. With nimble footwork, they had seen the gap and taken it. It was a brilliant move.

31

It's half an hour to midnight. We're at Governor's Lookout Camp on the Rock, muffled against the cold. A crowd has assembled near the bonfire built by the boy scouts. Lights flicker in the distance, along the scythe of the bay and around the straggling rosette of Algeciras. The mood is expectant; the talk and laughter has a thrilling edge. Mrs Rook and Jill are as excited as children, smiling and chattering and rubbing their hands together for warmth. The governor and prime minister are due any minute. Then the beacon will blaze.

The pub closed early to allow everyone to prepare for the New Year celebrations. As I walked back along Main Street, through the Southport Gates and up the side of the Rock, I took a hard look at myself and saw a poor Robinson Crusoe figure marooned in a colonial backwater and desperate for news of home. Why don't you go back if you miss it so much? I should have asked myself. And I would have been hard pressed to provide an answer.

But writing this book has helped. With every page completed, I have laid certain memories to rest, although it hasn't been easy. I witnessed so few of the events of the early part of the story that I have had to patch them together from what Sally said or wrote in the newspaper, or from what I read in her diaries. Later, the jigsaw grew easier as I became one of the bigger pieces, as it were, nudging Sally and Alice into the background. But on the periphery or not, they are very much part of the picture. Some would say they are the picture. Or at least Alice is.

The crowd is clapping. The governor and chief minister have arrived. Jill and Mrs Rook have grasped my coat sleeves and are peering towards the pyramid of kindling. The crowd hushes. The governor and chief minister explain that the bonfire will be one of a thousand beacons lit across Europe as a symbol of goodwill and urge us all to play our part in the kinship of mankind. Then it is midnight and the matches flare. Flames wreath upwards, crackling.

Cheers erupt as the blaze lights up the night. Ships' hooters drone in the harbour. In the distance in Spain, the next beacon is visible. But across the straits, Africa is lost in darkness.

Glossary

baas: boss, master (Afrikaans)

babouches: slippers

bakkie: light truck, pick-up (Afrikaans)

bibi: mistress, madam (Swahili)

brochette: kebab

bwana: mister, sir (Swahili)

Coloured: South African of mixed descent

couscous: steamed semolina (from Arabic kouskous)

dixie: mess tin (from Hindi)

djellaba: wool or cotton hooded outer garment

donder: to beat up, thrash (Afrikaans)

dreadlocks: matted, braided hair

gogga: insect (Afrikaans from Nama Xo Xo)

induna: headman, supervisor (Zulu)

majoun: a paste made with cannabis

nkosaan: master, sir, of a young person (from Zulu nkosana)

numzana: master, sir, of an older person (Zulu)

ou: chap, guy, fellow (Afrikaans; plural: ous)

outjie: 'little chap', slightly contemptuous (Afrikaans)

rastaman: Rastafarian

shamba: plantation (Swahili)

souk: market or market quarter

strandloper: prehistoric coastal race of South Africa, possible forerunner of Bushmen and Hottentots (Afrikaans)

ville nouvelle: modern, formerly colonial, quarter (French)

zenana: part of house reserved for women and girls (Hindi zanana)

THE ARROWING OF THE CANE

'Close to Doris Lessing's *The Grass is Singing* and to Nadine Gordimer's *The Conversationist* in its exploration of one individual consciousness and its relationship with Africa, the Africa which it loves but to which it doesn't belong ... as good and as skilful as either of those two novels ... The voice here is riveting, the observation exact, the writing as good as anything which has come out of white South Africa ... an important novel.'
COLM TOIBIN *Irish Sunday Independent*

'Examines the white man's burden without making heavy weather of it ... all the more accomplished for its painful ambivalence.'
DAVID PROFUMO *Daily Telegraph*

'Must rank amongst the finest descriptive writing to come out of this country.'
HEATHER MACKIE *Cape Times*

'Mr Conyngham has deftly fashioned a metaphor for a country facing its own three o'clock in the morning of the soul.'
MICHAEL ROSS *New York Times Book Review*

The Arrowing of the Cane has something of classic status in Natal terms.'
WH BIZLEY *Natal University Focus*

'A brilliant novel.'
MAUREEN ISAACSON *Sunday Independent*

'Throughout, we feel the author's intimate knowledge of the situation in both rural and urban Africa and also the richness of his language. His book is a virtual poem, an ode to nature, to the fauna and flora of the black continent.'
NADEZDA OBRADOVIC *World Literature Today*

9 780648 728245